TURNING A TRICK . . .

"I'd say you enjoyed pretty damn well," Fargo remarked, as, once again, his eyes roved over her beautiful body.

A tiny mask of satisfaction slipped over her face as she pushed up on her elbows. "But it's done, now. I matched her offer," Amber said.

"What offer?" Fargo asked casually as he pulled on his pants.

He watched her stiffen. "Jody Tanner's offer," she slid out.

"I never said she made me an offer," he answered.

Amber's eyes flashed fury. "You bastard. You tricked me," she shouted.

Fargo laughed. "You tricked yourself. You so mad because you gave it away for the wrong reason?"

D1553538

Exciting Westerns by Jon Sharpe from SIGNET

THE TRAILSMAN

18

CRY THE CHEYENNE

by
Jon Sharpe

A SIGNET BOOK
NEW AMERICAN LIBRARY
TIMES MIRROR

NAL BOOKS ARE AVAILABLE AT QUANTITY DISCOUNTS WHEN USED TO PROMOTE PRODUCTS OR SERVICES. FOR INFORMATION PLEASE WRITE TO PREMIUM MARKETING DIVISION, THE NEW AMERICAN LIBRARY, INC., 1633 BROADWAY, NEW YORK, NEW YORK 10019.

The first chapter of this book appeared in *Ride the Wild Shadow,* the seventeenth volume in this series.

SIGNET TRADEMARK REG. U.S. PAT. OFF. AND FOREIGN COUNTRIES
REGISTERED TRADEMARK—MARCA REGISTRADA
HECHO EN CHICAGO, U.S.A.

SIGNET, SIGNET CLASSICS, MENTOR, PLUME, MERIDIAN and NAL BOOKS are published by The New American Library, Inc., 1633 Broadway, New York, New York 10019

First Printing, June, 1983

1 2 3 4 5 6 7 8 9

PRINTED IN THE UNITED STATES OF AMERICA

The Trailsman

Beginnings ... they bend the tree and they mark the man. Skye Fargo was born when he was eighteen. Terror was his midwife, vengeance his first cry. Killing spawned Skye Fargo, ruthless, cold-blooded murder. Out of the acrid smoke of gunpowder still hanging in the air, he rose, cried out a promise never forgotten.

The Trailsman, they began to call him, all across the West: searcher, scout, hunter, the man who could see where others only looked, his skills for hire but not his soul, the man who lived each day to the fullest, yet trailed each tomorrow. Skye Fargo, the Trailsman, the seeker who could take the wildness of a land and the wanting of a woman and make them his own.

The Cheyenne land,
north of Medicine Bow,
where the Horse Creek River
crossed into the Nebraska Territory.

1

The big man with the lake-blue eyes surveyed the carnage with a face that seemed carved out of stone—a chiseled, handsome, intense face. He stood apart from the others, had ridden over the hillock only a few minutes before the cavalry troop had reached the spot. The girl and the old man had come along later, and the big black-haired man's eyes moved slowly over the scene, the bodies that lay on the ground like so many battered doll figures, arms and legs askew, some half-draped over the sides of the two charred Conestoga wagons. He made a sour face and the disgust stabbed into the pit of his stomach.

He had seen it too many times, knew the look of it, the feel of it, the smell of it. This was the same but different, and he turned his eyes to the cavalry patrol, a ten-man troop all shine and polish, including their young faces. The lieutenant picked his way amid the stink of death, his face held stiff.

The big black-haired man had seen the lieutenant before, too, just as he had viewed the scene before. Other times and other places. The same but different, he grunted silently once again. The young officer was made of stiff formality, newly weaned on army manuals and rule-book tactics, long on new learning and short on old wisdom.

The big man's eyes sought out the girl. Good-looking she was, he noted, hair the color of new wheat, eyes a soft, misty blue, an almost-pert nose, nice mouth with the lower lip fuller than the upper. She wore the new-wheat hair pulled back, but it made her face more young-girl-like than severe the way pulled-back hair does with most women. Her lime shirt pushed out in smooth fullness and she sat her gray mare with ease. He saw her grow ashen when she rode up, and he thought she was going to be sick. Not that he'd have blamed her. The men were riddled with arrows, their bodies resembling pincushions. The women lay half-naked, legs stretched wide, thighs smeared with blood and dirt where they'd been used before being killed. Five children lay with their heads bashed in. But the girl had pulled herself together and faced the scene, and he gave her credit for that.

His eyes swung from the girl as he heard the lieutenant's voice call out. "When did you say you got here, mister?" the officer asked.

"Five minutes before you did," the big man answered.

The lieutenant squatted down beside a lifeless form both bloodied and shot through with arrows. "What's your name, mister?" he asked without looking up.

"Fargo," the big man replied.

The lieutenant stood up and bit out his words. "The rotten, murdering savages," he said.

"The Cheyenne?" Fargo heard the girl ask.

"Of course," the lieutenant snapped grimly.

"No."

The big man let the single word drop softly from his lips and saw the others turn to him. The girl's eyes studied him, the lieutenant frowning.

"No?" the young officer echoed. "Of course it was the Cheyenne. You don't know much about Indians, do you, mister?" he said.

"I know enough, more than I want to know," Fargo said almost wearily.

"Then I suggest you learn some more. These are Cheyenne arrows with Cheyenne markings on them, Indian pony tracks all over the ground," the lieutenant said. He reached down, picked up a piece of torn pouch, a design cut into it. "And this carries a Cheyenne design pattern," he said, unable to keep from sounding smugly paternal. "The Cheyenne, no doubt about it, the stinking, bloodthirsty savages," he added darkly.

Fargo let a long sigh push from his powerful chest. "No." he said wearily, and turned to his horse, a stunning Ovaro, jet-black fore and hind quarters, a gleaming white midsection.

"The Cheyenne, Fargo," he heard the lieutenant call. "You better learn your Indians if you want to ride this territory and keep your scalp."

"Yes, sir, Lieutenant, I'll work on it," Fargo said as he pulled himself onto the Ovaro. He saw the girl's mist-blue eyes watching him, a tiny furrow crossing her brow. He touched the brim of his hat to her as he turned the horse.

The lieutenant shot a glance at the sun starting to dip over the horizon. "I'll leave a two-man guard overnight. It's too late to get a burial detail out here now. We'll tend to it in the morning," Fargo heard him say to the girl. "You need an escort back, Miss Jody?"

"No," the girl answered.

Jody, Fargo muttered silently. It fit her—a good, no-nonsense name, strong yet feminine. He let the pinto amble slowly away and felt the girl's eyes following him. On the other side of the hillock the scene of death was out of sight. Only the smell of charred wood followed him. He frowned as he slowly rode across the rabbit-brush-studded land. Strange, he grunted to himself, but he rode on. He'd no taste for getting into it, whatever it was.

He'd gone but a quarter of a mile or so, his eyes scanning the land to find a place for the night before the sun went down, when he heard the hoofbeats coming up fast behind him. He turned in the saddle to see the girl, the old man following behind on an old horse. Fargo continued to slowly walk the pinto until she reined up alongside him. Her soft, mist-blue eyes could turn sharp, he saw as she studied him, watched her take in his intense, chiseled handsomeness with approval.

"You still hold to what you said back there?" she asked.

He nodded.

"Why?" she prodded.

"My reasons," he answered.

"Let's hear them," she said.

He shook his head. "I said my piece."

"You said one word, no reasons, nothing else," she corrected him tartly.

"I'm not getting into it more," he said calmly. He let a small smile edge his lips as he took in her bristling dissatisfaction with him. "How come you followed me

12

all the way here to ask that? Don't you believe the lieutenant? He had a whole passel of reasons," Fargo said.

"He did," she snapped. "Lieutenant Richardson is a bright, fine young officer."

"You know him," Fargo grunted.

"Yes, I do," she said. "Frankly, I don't know why I followed you. Something about you, about the way you said that one word."

"It didn't impress the lieutenant any," Fargo commented.

"Maybe it shouldn't have impressed me, either," she tossed at him. "Maybe Lieutenant Richardson was right about your having a lot to learn."

"Maybe." Fargo smiled pleasantly.

The furrow on her brow had become an angry frown. But she remained one very good-looking package. "Are you going to give me a reason, dammit?" she snapped.

"I read the wind," he said.

She pulled the gray mare in a tight circle. "Bastard," she threw back as she cantered away.

The old man, a lined, narrow face on a spare, narrow body, followed after her at once.

Fargo smiled as he thought about the girl. Mist-blue eyes had a banked fire behind them. She'd be worth the knowing, and he wondered why she was so interested in what had happened. More than the usual, passing interest in the violence of this land. It was the Cheyenne land, he knew, and the Cheyenne could make savagery into a fine art. But he'd not get into it more. He had things to do, appointments to keep.

The dusk was nearly night and he rode to a stand of white cedar and halted, unsaddled the pinto, and laid

13

out his bedroll. The night stayed warm and he un- dressed to his shorts, placed the holster with the big Colt .45 in it alongside him. His hand rested lightly on it as he turned on his side and quickly slept, the rolling prairie stretched out below him and the distant call of a wolf his lullaby.

Fargo had long ago learned to sleep like the mountain cat, his subconscious forever alert, intuition and instinct awake just below his dulled surface senses. His eyes were still closed and he felt the dawn wind when it came, let himself return to sleep a while longer when he woke, unmoving, his eyes snapping open. He listened to the silence, heard it broken by the sound of a horse, the faint jingle of rein chains. No Cheyenne pony, he grunted, but his hand slowly drew the Colt from the holster. He turned, rose on one elbow, the big Colt ready to fire when he saw the gray mare moving up the incline toward the cedars. The gun was still in his hand when the girl halted before him, new-wheat hair pale gold in the early sun. He saw her eyes travel across his hard-muscled body, linger on the powerful deltoid muscles, linger longer on the flat, hard abdomen where it disappeared into his shorts.

" 'Morning, Jody,'' he said evenly, and saw the surprise in her eyes. "That's what Lieutenant Richard- son called you," Fargo said.

"It's Jody," she said, almost smiling. "You can put the gun away."

He nodded, leaned over, and returned the Colt to the holster. He pushed himself to his feet and watched her eyes move over his near-naked body again. "You come out here at dawn to ask questions again?" he said. "You'll be getting the same answers."

14

"I don't think so," she said as he pulled on trousers. He looked up from buttoning his pants to see the heavy Dragoon Colt in her hand. "Move away from your holster," she said.

He eyed the gun in her grip. "You don't want to play with those things, honey," he said soothingly. "They can go off."

"I know how to make them go off," she said. "Move aside." He obeyed and she dismounted, kept the gun steady on him. She scooped up his gun belt and slung it around her saddle horn. "Finish dressing," she ordered.

"What the hell's in you?" Fargo asked as he pulled on his shirt.

"Those wagons," she said. "You're going back there with me right now, before the lieutenant's burial detail gets there. Saddle up."

He lifted his saddle, put it on the Ovaro. "Why?" he asked.

"You're going to show me why you said it wasn't the Cheyenne," she snapped.

"Thought you'd decided the lieutenant was right about me not knowing anything," Fargo said.

"You know, damn you," she threw back. "You know. I can feel it inside."

He threw a glance at her. The big Dragoon Colt hadn't wavered a fraction and he swung up on the Ovaro. She moved the gray mare a few paces behind him.

"Let's go," she said. "You're going to give me reasons, chapter and verse. No bullshit about reading the wind this time."

He shrugged. He'd tell her the truth. He'd give her that much. She had the guts to follow through on her intuition and he could admire that. He watched the dawn sun lift over the horizon, tossed her a smile. "The early bird gets the answers," he said. Her eyes softened, but he saw that she kept the gun steady. He hurried along the flatland, and the hillock came into sight. He saw her draw a deep breath and follow after him.

2

The smell had slid into stench and Fargo watched the girl's lips grow thin as she held back taking deep breaths. The two troopers left on guard had moved to the far end of the hillock, downwind, and recognized the girl and himself, Fargo saw, as they watched his approach. They were content to watch from a distance and Fargo crested the hillock, moved down the other side, and felt the anger and disgust rise inside him once again at the grisly scene. He swung from the saddle, eyed Jody, saw she kept the gun steady.

"Talk," she bit out, and Fargo moved to the figures of two men draped over the charred side of one of the Conestogas.

"Arrows," he said laconically, and saw her frown at him. "They can be like words. They tell their own story."

"What do these tell?" she pressed.

"Too many," Fargo grunted.

"Too many?" she echoed with a frown.

"It takes a long time for an Indian to make an arrow. He doesn't waste them. He wouldn't riddle a body like this. The Cheyenne would never do this with their arrows," Fargo said. "And most of these were shot at close range. The Cheyenne would have shot one or two from a distance."

He watched the girl's misty-blue eyes grow darker as she stared at him. "What about the markings?" she asked. "Lieutenant Richardson said the arrows had Cheyenne markings in Cheyenne colors."

Fargo uttered a wry grunt, broke one of the arrows in two, and held up the feathered end where three bands of color circled the shaft. "Cheyenne colors, all right, only these have been painted on," he said. "The Cheyenne use dyes—marigold, turmeric, henna, black walnut. They rub them into the wood with a buffalo-tail brush. The finished result is the same but different."

He saw her eyes grow rounder as she listened. She gestured to the piece of torn pouch on the ground. "What about the design on that?" she questioned.

He glanced at the object where it lay. "Cheyenne design, but made by a white man's cutting tool, a knife, probably. The Cheyenne tools are flint-sharpened. They leave a thicker line in the leather."

"They have plenty of white men's knives now," she said.

Fargo leaned over, picked up the torn piece of pouch. "True enough, but they use them differently," he said, pressed the markings on the leather with his fingers, spreading the lines apart. "They don't cut as deeply as this and they make one steady cut. This was made by a series of small cuts, somebody copying from a Cheyenne design. It was left on purpose to add to the picture," he said.

She blinked, her lips tight, gestured to the ground. "These prints . . . unshod Indian ponies," she muttered.

He squatted down beside the hoofprints. "Unshod, all right, but no Indian ponies. Look here, that one's as big a print as your gray mare would make. The others, too. They're all too big. Not a one is an Indian pony." He rose, shook his head with wry admiration. "They did it well. They didn't miss a bet. They did it more than good enough to fool most people," he said.

"But not you," she said.

He shrugged.

"Why not you?" she pressed.

"Seeing what other men don't see is my business. That's why they call me the Trailsman," he said.

Her eyes stayed on him, searching his handsome, chiseled face. "You said you read the wind. I believe it now. I'm more than impressed," she said.

"Didn't do it to impress you," he said, swinging onto the Ovaro. "I figured anyone wants reasons this bad ought to have them. I'll take my gun now."

She moved the mare closer, handed him the gun belt, and watched as he put it on.

"Jody the only name you've got?" he asked casually.

"Jody Tanner," she said.

"Why are you so interested in this, Jody Tanner?" he questioned.

"This is the fourth wagon train massacred by the Cheyenne in the last three weeks," she said. "Or what we thought was the Cheyenne."

"Maybe the others were the real thing. This one wasn't," he said.

"The others were all like this. I went with Lieutenant

19

Richardson on one and he told me about the others, everybody riddled with arrows," she said.

"You didn't answer my question," Fargo said. "Only you came after me for answers. Why?"

She paused for a half-second. "My brother was killed in the attack on the first of the four wagon trains," she said.

"Good-enough reason," Fargo commented as he watched her. She had gone into private thoughts, the frown still knitting her brow. "You've ideas?" he asked.

"About what?" she said, pulling away from her thoughts.

"About why anyone would be attacking these wagon trains, butchering up men, women, and children, and going to a lot of trouble to make it seem the Cheyenne," Fargo said.

"Maybe," she answered.

He shrugged, started to move the Ovaro up over the hillock. "Pretty damn rotten, whatever it is," he commented as he started away. He heard her following as he rode down the other side of the hillock.

"Wait," she called, and he paused, watched her come up to him, draw a deep breath, and her shirt filled nicely with smooth curves. "You found out this much. You could find out more," she said.

"Such as?" he questioned.

"Who's doing it?" she said.

"You said you had ideas," he returned.

"Ideas aren't enough. I need proof. You could get me the proof and I'll see to the rest," Jody Tanner said.

He tossed her a grin. "You saying you're taking my word on this over the lieutenant's?" he asked.

She returned a slightly acid glance. "I guess I am," she said.

"That won't sit well with your soldier boy," Fargo remarked.

"He's not my soldier boy," Jody Tanner snapped. "And that will be my problem, won't it?"

He nodded mildly and decided there was steel beneath the new-wheat hair and misty-blue eyes.

"I'll hire you to get me proof," Jody said.

"Sorry," Fargo answered.

Her frown was instant. "Why not?" she demanded.

"I'm hired. That's what's brought me out here," Fargo told her, and the letter in his pocket seemed to rustle its own reminder. "I've come to take a wagon train through Cheyenne territory," he said, swinging from the Ovaro to adjust the left stirrup.

"Cancel out. I'll double whatever they're paying you," Jody said, dismounting to stand beside him impatiently.

Fargo's eyes narrowed as he studied the girl. She was more than determined, an urgency lining her tone. "Sorry. I made an agreement. I don't go back on my word," he said.

"Dammit, who's involved? You won't have to go back on your word. I'll buy out your agreement with them," Jody persisted. She saw the questions in his eyes. "Somebody's going to pay for killing my brother," she said quickly—almost too quickly, he mused silently. Yet he didn't worry the thought. It was reason enough and he'd nothing to question her grief. "Who hired you?" Jody pressed.

"Holloway," he said.

He watched Jody's misty-blue eyes stare at him, her mouth fall open. "Amber Holloway?" she breathed.

"She wrote the letter. Got my name from a good friend," Fargo said.

Jody Tanner continued to stare at him, slowly pulled her lovely lips closed. "I told you I had ideas," she murmured.

It was Fargo's turn to find a frown digging into his brow. "Amber Holloway? Behind the fake Cheyenne attacks?" he muttered, and Jody Tanner nodded. Her eyes met his stare. "You'd best have good reasons for that kind of talk, honey," he said.

"I've reasons," she answered.

"Name some," he snapped.

"The attacks on the wagons had to be done by a fair-size band. The Holloway place is the only one around with enough hands to put on that kind of attack," Jody said.

"That doesn't cut far. Gunhands can be hired by anybody. Why would they go around attacking wagon trains as the Cheyenne?" Fargo pressed.

"Amber Holloway's not about to have anyone else settling near here," Jody Tanner said. "She's bought claim to a lot of the land around her, but she wants more. Only she's not ready to take on more yet. She wants the land left for her till she's ready. The only way to do that is to make sure nobody new settles in."

Fargo's frown stayed on the girl and he knew the skepticism showed in his eyes.

"It fits, don't you see that?" Jody insisted quickly. "They see to it that no one settles any of the land around here and the Cheyenne get the blame. It's called ruthlessness and greed."

Fargo turned her words in his mind. He couldn't embrace them—not yet, anyway. But he couldn't just

22

dismiss them, either. He'd seen what greed could do to people.

Jody Tanner's voice cut into his thoughts. "Working for Amber Holloway would be taking blood money. Forget your agreement with her. Work for me. Get me the proof. Stop any more wagon-train massacres," she said.

"I don't just forget about agreements I make," Fargo said. "You've tossed out hard words, but hard words can come out of feuding, fighting, or just plain jealousy."

"You're saying you don't believe me." She glared.

"I'm saying I don't know you or Amber Holloway, and I'm not passing judgments now. I'll keep my meeting with her and see what I think after that," Fargo said.

Jody Tanner tossed her head in a derisive gesture, the new-wheat hair snapping out to catch the sun. "I know what you'll think after that. You'll go along with her. She'll sweet-talk you into it," Jody snapped.

"Sweet-talk me?" Fargo smiled. "I'll take it over six-gun talk anytime. I was beginning to think you never heard about it."

He saw the misty-blue eyes take on an angry smolder. She took a step forward and he found himself surprised as her mouth reached up to his, pressed softly, a sweet honey taste to her. She held as he opened his lips, began to respond, felt the tiny tip of her tongue, and then she pulled away, stepped back.

"Very nice," he murmured, and a tiny glint of satisfaction touched her eyes.

"Still think I never heard about sweet-talk?" she speared.

"You proving or promising?" Fargo asked.

"Maybe a little of both," she said. She turned, swung onto the gray mare.

"I'll keep that in mind," he remarked.

"I'm sure you will," she said, and looked smugly confident. "I'll wait to hear from you, after you've done your thinking," she said, and let a tartness creep into her voice.

"Where?" he asked.

"Ride past those bur oaks in the distance and head due west. You'll find a road. Take it as far as it goes," she said, and turned the mare to ride away, new-wheat hair swinging out behind her, soft, smooth curves under her blouse rising and falling in unison.

He watched till she disappeared from sight, and the taste of her lips was still with him as he swung onto the pinto. She had quickly become a lovely question mark. And a very determined one, he added silently. Of course, her brother's death would supply reason enough to seek out truth and cry for vengeance. Yet his senses had picked up something more that he couldn't pin down. He shook away idle speculation and turned the pinto southwest toward a series of three ridges, as per the instructions in the letter in his pocket. He'd kept careful track of the days he'd spent in the saddle and he was arriving exactly on the day his own letter had said he'd arrive.

He rode slowly and his eyes automatically swept the hills, the thick summer foliage: a lush cover of snowberries, their cottony, white clusters brilliant against the deep-green, soft leaves; and along one ridge, a carpet of viny, blue-flowered vetches. Plenty of good tree cover, he noted grimly, walnut and white birch, hop hornbeam and alder, and higher on the hills, Douglas fir and balsam. But he saw no movement in the lush greenery, caught no flash of bronzed bodies, and he halted beside a thick black oak as the noon sun began to dip in the sky. He dismounted, let the pinto graze as he lunched on pemmican from his saddlebag.

The events of the last twenty-four hours mingled in his thoughts—the brutality of the attack on the wagon train, the deception written in blood, Jody Tanner and her accusations—and he felt the uneasiness inside him. He fought it away. It was too soon to give in to suspicions and doubts. But he felt the irritation as it roiled inside him. He'd come to take on a danger-filled task. Death was always a constant companion in Indian country. But it had been a straightforward task, direct and uncomplicated, shadowed only by danger, and now it was no longer simple. Suddenly strange questions prodded each other and there was a sourness, a dark and ugly undercurrent.

Maybe Jody Tanner was all wrong in her accusations, he pondered. Maybe they were fashioned of unwarranted assumptions fed by jealousy and God knows what, he snorted silently. But the brutal massacre of the wagon train swam into his mind at once. That had been no unfounded assumption. That had been death wearing a mask, a Cheyenne mask.

He rose, irritated, refusing to speculate further. Perhaps it would all go away, the reasons and the answers left to others to find. That would suit him just fine. He had come to take a wagon train through the Cheyenne country, and that was task enough.

He rode on till he spied the ridge of balsams the letter had told him to watch for, and he spurred the pinto up to the sweet-sharp aroma of the tall evergreens and followed a line that wove up and down the ridge, through sudden rocky protruberances and down toward a stand of timber. He had almost reached the timber when he saw the horseman, a lone figure, moving out from behind a tall rock overgrown with goblet lichen. He reined up and watched the man move down to block his path, took in a thin figure wearing a dark checked shirt. The horseman moved toward him and Fargo saw a long face, a four-day stubble on the chin, pale eyes, and cheeks deeply lined, a face made of a kind of wary sadness.

Fargo's hand moved to rest easily at the side of his holster as the horseman came nearer and halted.

"You heading to the Holloway place, mister?" the man asked.

"I might be," Fargo answered carefully.

"You the one they call the Trailsman?" the man questioned.

"I am." Fargo nodded.

"You're right on time. I heard you were expected to show today, but most folks don't make it on time out here," the man said.

"I'm not most folks," Fargo said.

"I heard that, too," the man said, and Fargo let his eyes take in the figure again. Nothing changed his first impression, the wary-sad face, the eyes that were more troubled than hostile. He noted the man kept his hands atop the saddle horn. "Been waiting around two days," the man offered. "Watching for you, waiting."

"You work at the Holloway place?" Fargo asked.

"Until a few days back," the man said.

"You quit or get fired?" Fargo asked with sudden sharpness.

"I pulled out," the man answered.

"You've got a name, mister?" Fargo asked.

"Bowdy, Sam Bowdy," the man said.

"What's brought you out here waiting for me, Bowdy?" the big black-haired man questioned.

"I've things you'll want to hear," Sam Bowdy answered.

"Why me?" Fargo pressed.

"Because I've heard of you and the territory marshal won't be this way till the end of the month, and I just couldn't stand by anymore," Sam Bowdy said.

Fargo studied the man's face, peered into the sadwary countenance. Sam Bowdy carried something heavy inside him, he decided.

"Besides, from what I heard about you, I figured you'd want to know," the man said.

"I'm listening," Fargo said.

Sam Bowdy took a deep breath and the sadness in his face seemed to grow deeper. He opened his mouth to speak just as the shot exploded in the hills. Instead of words, a torrent of blood, bone, and teeth spewed from his mouth as the bullet slammed through the back of his head and out through his mouth.

Fargo's reaction was instinctive and quick as he flung himself sideways from the saddle. He hit the ground on his side, rolled, glimpsed Sam Bowdy's faceless body topple from the horse. Fargo halted against a rock, and his eyes leaped to the high ground beyond, saw a horse's brown rump disappearing up a passageway.

Fargo cursed softly to himself as he leaped to his feet, swung onto the pinto, the big Colt .45 in one hand. He sent the black-and-white horse into a full gallop, climbing the steep slope of land where the rifleman had vanished. He took a very steep grade, aware the pinto could make it, and saved precious seconds. He leaned forward in the saddle to add balance as the pinto pulled upward, slipped once but recovered instantly. He felt the powerful hindquarters knotting, pushing, and the deep blow of air as the horse reached the top of the slope. Fargo halted, his eyes sweeping the hills, and he spotted the horseman ahead and to the right, driving his horse upward along narrow hill trails. The single shot had clearly been an assassination, Fargo grunted. Someone didn't want Sam Bowdy to talk to him.

He drove the pinto through a narrow crevice that let him cut away another half-minute, emerged at the other end to see the horseman more clearly. The man wore a wide-brimmed dark-gray hat, and Fargo saw him half-turn, toss a glance backward. Fargo saw a young face under the wide brim and then the man turned away, concentrated on pushing his horse upward to where the timber gave way to boulders of gray slate honeycombed with passages.

Fargo raced the pinto forward, followed the killer as the man disappeared into a space between two clifflike boulders. He rode into the space, reined to a halt just long enough to listen and catch the sound of the fleeing horseman. His mouth formed a thin line as he nodded to himself, sent the pinto up a side passage of steep, slippery stone, but when he emerged he had closed again on the killer. He glimpsed the rider making his way higher through the rocks, spurred the pinto on, and raced up another narrow passage.

He'd neared the top when he reined up, listened, ears straining, but suddenly the sound of racing hoofbeats had vanished. Fargo dived out of the saddle just as the shot rang out, echoing through the rocky terrain. He saw the bullet strike the rock just back of where he'd been in the saddle, and he flung himself onto his stomach, the Colt in hand, his eyes sweeping the rocks. Another shot rang out and bits of gray shale flew into the air a few inches from his head.

The killer was firing from an opening between two jagged boulders, he saw, and he pushed himself sideways to stay out of the line of fire as he began to crawl forward. He halted as the sound of hoofbeats echoed suddenly. "Goddamn," he spat out aloud as he leaped to his feet, vaulted onto the pinto, and gave chase again.

The man had fled once more, this time straight upward along a wide pathway between shale formations. Fargo holstered the Colt and reached back to draw the big Sharps rifle from its saddle holster. He lifted the rifle into position as he raced the pinto forward. He saw the killer vanish between rocks, reappear where one boulder dipped down.

Fargo started to tighten his finger on the trigger of the rifle when the fleeing assassin vanished again. Cursing softly, Fargo spurred the pinto forward through the pathway, came out behind the fleeing horseman, close enough to be well within rifle range. The rider came into view again, and Fargo slowed the pinto, brought the big Sharps up, and fired. The shot slammed into the rocks just left of the horseman and the man made his mistake. He reined up, turned to fire back, but Fargo had the rifle still at his shoulder. He fired again and saw the man double over in the saddle, grasp his left thigh, almost topple from the horse. He clung to his seat and dug heels into the horse to send it racing along a side path.

Again Fargo sent the pinto into pursuit and saw the rocks come to an end in a thick stand of blue spruce. He saw the assassin, riding doubled up in pain, rein to a halt at the edge of the spruce and slide from the saddle, standing on his right leg. Fargo fired the big Sharps as he raced forward, taking a moment to aim, and he saw the man spin, fall, his right arm suddenly turning red. He saw the man roll into the trees, turned the pinto sharply to the right, and ducked low as a volley of wild shots sprayed the air.

Fargo half-ran, half-dived up along the other edge of the stand of spruce, staying inside the tree line but moving up a steep incline. He halted, dropped to one knee, and let his eyes slowly move across the forest floor just below where he rested. He found the figure in moments, the man resting on his side, a rifle cradled in the crook of his good arm. He bled heavily from his left thigh, and Fargo watched him tie a bandanna around his right arm.

"You can talk and stay alive, mister," Fargo called over the barrel of the big Sharps.

The man rolled in sudden panic, went onto his back, and fired at the sound of the voice that had cut through the forest of spruce. The shot went a foot over the Trailsman's head, and Fargo sighted along the gun barrel, fired, saw the bullet slam into the shoulder of the arm with the bandanna on it.

"Ow, Jesus," he heard the man cry in pain, twist and turn, one hand clapped to his shattered shoulder. He tried to pull himself under a heavy overhang of foliage.

Fargo let him take cover that was really no cover at all. "Why'd you kill Sam Bowdy, mister?" Fargo called. Through the spruce needles he saw the man crawl forward again, using his good arm and his one good leg to pull himself forward.

Fargo waited, let the figure below pass through a space between branches. He aimed, fired again, and the man screamed in pain as his other calf bone shattered. Fargo watched him roll, pull his leg up in pain. "You're going to talk, mister, if I have to shoot you apart piece by piece," Fargo called.

He listened to the man's harsh, pain-racked breathing as he bled from all but one arm. Once again the man turned, used his remaining good arm to pull himself forward. Fargo frowned, watched him crawl to a place where two spruce had fallen to form a protective pyramid. He almost felt admiration for the man, but he was a killer, an assassin, he reminded himself. The man had shot Sam Bowdy through the back of the head in cold-blooded murder.

"You going to talk?" he called again, and saw the man halt in front of the two fallen trees.

"All right, gimme a minute," the man rasped through pain-filled breaths.

Fargo stayed silent, waited, watched through the thick spruce branches. He saw the man pull himself up to a sitting position against the fallen trees, using his one remaining good arm. He rested, the wide-brimmed hat obscuring his face, but Fargo heard his half-groaned breathing, pain in every rasped intake of air.

Fargo lowered the rifle a fraction. "Talk, mister," he called. "I don't figure to wait much longer."

The man nodded, used his good arm to push himself up straighter. With a sudden gasped cry of pain, he pushed down hard with his arm, flung himself backward over the fallen log.

"Damn," Fargo swore as he brought the rifle up, took quick aim, and fired. The shot slammed into the man's remaining good arm at the point of the shoulder as he fell behind the tree.

"Ow . . . goddamn, oh, Jesus," he heard the man scream as he disappeared behind the thick log.

Fargo scrambled down the slope, his lips drawn back. "You want to do it the hard way, mister," he said as he reached the level ground. He crouched, started toward the pyramid formed by the two fallen trees. The man's breathing had grown harsher, a rattling, pain-racked sound.

Fargo moved forward cautiously as only the rasping, groaning sound of his quarry's breathing filled the spruce forest. He had neared the fallen trees, started to make his way to one end to circle around, when the shot resounded. Again Fargo's reaction was swift and instinctive as he dropped low, half-rolled, came up with the rifle ready to fire. He lay motionless for a moment, felt the frown pressing across his forehead. There was only silence in the forest.

Fargo waited, felt the frown press more deeply into his brow. The rasping, groaning breaths had stopped, and Fargo rose carefully, listened. The man could have held his pain-filled breathing for a few seconds but no longer. Fargo rose, heard the curse whisper inside himself as he ran forward, the rifle ready to fire, skirted around the end of the fallen trees, and came to a halt.

"Damn," he breathed aloud as he gazed at the scene before him. The man lay sprawled beside the log, the right side of his temple blown in, his hand still clutching the gun in a lifeless grip.

3

Fargo straightened, walked to stare down at the man, the wide-brimmed hat now partially fallen aside. He saw a young face, sandy hair, and he dropped to one knee, went through the man's pockets, and found nothing. He rose, continued to frown down at the figure. The man had killed himself rather than be forced to talk. The frown stayed on Fargo's brow as he turned away, slowly walked back to the pinto.

He found himself more than surprised. The act had been out of character. Hired guns didn't kill themselves to avoid talking. That took something else, a kind of idealism or dedication. He pursued the thought. "Dedication" was a good word. And hired assassins were not the dedicated kind. Which meant that the killer had been more than a paid gunhand. Fargo tabled the thought and swung onto the pinto.

He returned to where Sam Bowdy's body lay, dismounted, and went through the man's pockets. They offered up the meager fare of a roving cowhand, a few gold pieces, some silver change, a half-dozen dollar bills, chewing tobacco, and an identification card that gave his birthplace as Kentucky. Sam Bowdy wouldn't see Boone's Trace again, Fargo murmured as he straightened up, found a length of branch, and slowly dug a shallow grave. He put the man's holster and boots beside the crude rock cross he formed atop the grave.

He climbed back onto the pinto and slowly rode away. He'd hardly spoken a dozen words with Sam Bowdy, but the man's murder stabbed at him. Sam Bowdy had waited to tell him something and been murdered for it. He'd find out about those unsaid words, Fargo muttered silently. He owed Sam Bowdy that much. He headed the pinto on toward the Holloway place as he wondered if perhaps Jody Tanner's accusations had more merit than he'd allowed them.

He rode down the high land to find the wide field of foxgrass Amber Holloway had described in her letter. On the other side of the field he rode down a passage and saw the ranch come into sight. He slowed, took in the size of the spread, fence posts marking boundaries almost as far as the eye could see across the flatland. Most of the land near the main house had been corralled into sections, and he noted a large number of steers and calves in the separated corrals. Three buildings stretched from the ranch house, two stables, the farthest away a bunkhouse.

Fargo rode the pinto into the ranch, past men transferring young steers from one corral to another, and drew idle glances as he rode by. He saw the young woman step from the stables as he reined to a halt. She came to him, stopped, her eyes taking in his chiseled handsomeness, the hard-muscled body that swung from the pinto with graceful ease.

"Fargo?" she asked, and he nodded. "I'm Amber Holloway," she said.

It was his turn to take in a soft-lined face, round cheeks, a pretty face with just the hint of self-indulgence in the full thrust of her lower lip. Long brown hair worn loose framed her oval face, and she had eyes that fit her name, a soft amber. Tall, long-waisted, she had a willowy figure a heavy, black riding skirt couldn't hide. Under a white blouse with puffed sleeves, soft, slightly pillowy contours formed.

"Nobody told me you'd be such a good-looking man," she said.

"I didn't figure anyone that looks like you," Fargo returned.

Her smile was quick and the amber eyes held a smoldering fire inside their tawny depths, he decided. "I'm glad you're here," Amber Holloway said, and he caught the hint of a soft drawl.

"Virginia?" he queried.

"Very good," she said, laughed in surprise, a soft, smooth sound. "You know your accents. But then you get around, don't you?"

"What are you doing way up here in this country?" Fargo asked.

"Running my ranch. Been here almost a year now. I got tired arguing with Daddy. I wanted my own place to run with my own ideas," she said.

Again, he saw a feline sultriness in the amber eyes and shifted his gaze for a moment to the man approaching: tall, hatless, sandy-color hair, not the average cowpoke's face, stronger, more determination in the heavy jaw. The man halted beside Amber Holloway, and Fargo noted he was well-muscled, with big shoulders and a deep chest. "This is Ken Dixon, my ranch foreman," Amber Holloway introduced.

Ken Dixon nodded pleasantly. "Have any trouble getting here? The Cheyenne have been on the warpath," he said.

"So I heard," Fargo said, keeping his voice casual. "Didn't see any, but I came onto a man named Sam Bowdy."

"You did?" Amber cut in. "Where?"

"Upland a ways. He was telling me he used to work for you when somebody shot him dead right in front of me and hightailed it instantly," Fargo said.

"Oh, my God," Amber gasped, and Fargo's glance at her was sharp. Her surprise seemed genuine, but then he didn't know how good an actress she might be, he reflected.

"Doesn't surprise me," Ken Dixon's voice answered, and Fargo rested his eyes on the foreman. "I let Sam Bowdy go a few days ago. He was too much of a problem, a constant troublemaker," Ken Dixon said. "He'd ride five miles into Hollowville and get into one scrape after another. He made enemies as naturally as a cow makes milk. Guess he made one too many."

"Guess so," Fargo agreed blandly. He'd tossed out the bait and gotten answers that seemed reasonable enough. Yet he thought of Sam Bowdy and a face that had none of the tight hardness of the born troublemaker. "Your wagons ready to roll?" he asked Amber, saw the ruefulness come into her face as she shot a quick glance at Ken Dixon.

"Afraid not. Our wagon teams have come up lame, every one of them," the foreman said. He saw the question form in the big black-haired man's lake-blue

36

eyes. "It turned chill the other night and somebody left the stable door open. They all came down stiff and lame. Caught a muscle chill of some kind," Dixon explained.

"How long do you figure before they'll be ready to go?" Fargo asked.

Ken Dixon half-shrugged. "Hard to say. A week, at least, maybe two," he answered.

Amber broke in. "Please come inside, Fargo, and I'll tell you more about the job and my ranch," she said, cast a glance at Ken Dixon. "Finish rotating the stock in the east forty," she said, and Dixon nodded, started to turn.

"Be seeing you, Fargo." He smiled pleasantly, and Fargo returned the gesture, started after Amber Holloway as she walked to the ranch house. He enjoyed watching her long-legged body move, definitely willowy, her rear moving with nice, firm tightness.

"Ken Dixon been with you long?" he asked as he followed her into the house.

"Daddy sent him with me as a present. He figured I'd need a good ranch foreman," Amber said, and Fargo took in the answer with a pleasant smile as he decided to move carefully, pick and choose questions. He found himself in a modest ranch house, simple pine furniture in the living room except for a leather settee.

"Drink?" Amber asked, halting before a small cabinet in a corner of the room.

"Sounds good. Bourbon?" Fargo said.

"Coming up," Amber answered, and Fargo eased his big frame into one of the pine chairs as Amber produced two glasses and a bottle of bourbon. She poured drinks and curled up on the settee across from him, but not before he saw a nicely turned calf and a smooth-lined leg above it. "I suppose you've been wondering what I'm going to move through Cheyenne territory," Amber said.

"A little." Fargo smiled as he sipped the bourbon and decided he'd had better. "I see you've got yourself a hell of a lot of land outside," he remarked casually.

"I need it for what I've been doing," Amber said. "I developed a new way of curing and tanning calfskin. My daddy kept saying I was all talk, so I took some money I had and left him back in Virginia. I came here and started my ranch."

"Why do you need so much land?" Fargo questioned mildly.

Amber took a long draw of her bourbon and Fargo watched it bring a pink flush to her round cheeks that made her look faintly as though she were a little girl wearing makeup incorrectly. "I've developed a new way of tanning calfskin which makes it softer, easier to cut and work with, and which keeps a more beautiful sheen to the hides. But I need a lot of calves and young steers in perfect condition. That means I need them away from older steers and kept in small groups, all to avoid their hides getting bruised, nicked, scraped, and gashed, which, as you know, happens in big herds."

"I take it your wagons will be carrying your hides," Fargo said.

"Exactly, hundreds of the finest hides ever seen, especially prepared, especially tanned by a method I've developed that uses egg white, honey, and cottonseed oil," Amber said. "I'm taking them into market in Omaha. Everything I have is in those hides. I want them to reach market, not the Cheyenne or any other thieving cutthroats. That's why I sent for you. I was told that if anyone can get my wagons through, you can do it.''

Fargo finished his bourbon and pulled himself to his feet. "I'll try," he said. "I'll stop back next week and see if your horses are ready to go."

Amber rose, the frown instant across her smooth brow. "Stop back?" she echoed. "You can stay here."

"No, I'll stop back. I came onto something I can do while I'm waiting," Fargo said.

"What?" Amber snapped out.

Fargo chose words slowly. "Met a gal on the way here, name of Jody Tanner. She wants me to scout some mountain land for her. You know her?" he asked mildly.

"Unfortunately I do," Amber snapped, and Fargo saw the amber eyes become copper fire.

"Sounds as though you don't care much for her," Fargo commented.

"She wanted some land I took over. She's said all kinds of ridiculous things about me since then. She's the kind who'll say or do anything to get her way," Amber Holloway said angrily.

"That's all none of my business." Fargo smiled. "She's offered good pay and I've no reason to pass it up."

Amber seemed to become taller as she grew angrier. "You certainly do," she snapped. "We've an agreement. You came here to trail for me, no one else. You can't just walk away from that."

Fargo's smile held, but an edge of frost came into it. Amber Holloway's sweet softness could take on instant authoritativeness, he saw. "You've a few things wrong,

Amber, honey," he said with quiet firmness. "First, I can do anything I damn well please. Second, you're not ready. And third, I'm not walking out on anything. I told you I'd stop back."

"I'll pay you for waiting here," Amber said, pulling the harshness from her tone.

"I take money for working, not waiting," Fargo said.

"I'll give you some chores to do if the idea upsets your sense of morality that much," she snapped, unable to hold the sarcasm from her voice.

Fargo let the smile slip from his face and the lake-blue eyes became blue quartz. "I'm no cowhand or stable boy," he growled, turned his back, and reached for the door.

"Wait," he heard Amber Holloway call. He halted, looked back, saw her biting her lip together. "I'm sorry," she said.

"I'll stop back next week," he said.

Her moment of remorse was short-lived as he saw the amber eyes become copper again. "Dammit, I don't see why you can't just wait here and be paid for it," she flung at him.

"I answered that," he said.

Her eyes narrowed as she stared at him. "So you did, and you know something, I don't buy that answer. I think there's something more."

"Such as?"

"Jody Tanner'd do anything to see I didn't get help. It's more than the pay she's offered, isn't it? She's promised you more. She's dangled it in front of you, hasn't she, promised to go to bed with you," Amber flung out in a combination of anger and smug satisfaction.

Fargo felt thoughts leapfrog inside himself, the possi- bilities suddenly opening up. He let a smile slowly slide across his face and watched Amber seize on it, gather it in to reinforce her angry assumptions.

"I knew it," she bit out. "Damn her. I knew it." Fargo said nothing, continued to let her feed on his smile and his silence. "I suppose you expect I'm going to match her offer," Amber threw at him, eyes flashing copper. Fargo stayed silent, gazed mildly back at her. "What would you do if I said I'd match her?" Amber questioned, a glower coming into her face, lower lip thrusting forward.

"You offering or asking?" Fargo answered.

"Asking," Amber snapped. He smiled, turned away, and pulled the door open. "Wait, where are you going?" she called quickly.

"Out to make camp before it gets dark," Fargo said. "I'll stop back next week."

"Maybe I want to talk some more," Amber said.

He allowed her another broad smile. "I'll camp at the edge of that stand of balsams," he said. "I'll pick a nice, cozy spot."

"Dammit, Fargo, we had an agreement," she called after him as he started through the doorway.

"We still have. Maybe a better one." He laughed and pulled the door closed after him. He'd just reached the pinto and started to swing into the saddle when Ken Dixon came over to him.

"You're not staying?" the man asked pleasantly enough.

"I'll be stopping back," Fargo said. He cast a glance at the ranch hands at their chores. "You bring your crew up with you?" he asked.

"Not all," Dixon said. "I took on four or five up here. All good men, except for Sam Bowdy."

"Get some liniment on those horses. I'm not much for waiting around," Fargo said as he turned the pinto.

"Using balm of gilead oil right now," the foreman said with a nod as Fargo rose from the ranch. The pinto moved with an easy gait onto the flatland and Fargo turned its head up toward the distant stand of balsams.

The night began to slide down the hillside, gray-purple that became almost black by the time he reached the trees. He found a small half-circle just back of the leading edge of the balsams and laid out his bedroll, comfortable on the soft forest floor, and watched a half-moon slowly climb into the night sky. He stretched out on his bedroll, removed his shirt in the warm night air, listened to the night sounds, and inhaled the sweet tang of the balsams. He half-dozed, determined not to let thoughts push at him until the night was over. He'd made a small wager with himself and was about to consider he'd lost as the half-moon rose high into the blue-black sky when he caught the faint sound, a horse blowing air, then the rattle of rein chains.

He rose, peered down the slope, picked out the rider slowly moving along the edge of the trees. "Over here," he called, and watched the horse shift directions, come toward him. The rider took form, long brown hair swaying loosely over her shoulders, her face unsmiling as she halted and slid from the horse.

He saw her glance move across his bare chest, appreciatively take in the smooth ripple of powerful pectoral muscles as he reached out and took her horse's reins, drew the mount to a tree, and secured him to a low branch.

She faced him, standing very tall and very straight, hands on her hips, and her white blouse drawn taut across her breasts in a smooth, unbroken curve. "I want to get one thing clear," Amber Holloway said. "There's only one reason I'm here. I need you to get my wagons through to Omaha. Everything I've worked for depends on getting those hides to market. Without that it's all been a waste and there are people waiting to see me fail. But that's none of your concern."

"That's right," he agreed mildly. "But you make it sound like you're not going to enjoy coming up here to see me."

"I didn't come up here to enjoy. It's called fighting fire with fire. I'm not letting someone like Jody Tanner ruin everything for me at the last minute," Amber said angrily.

"I said I'd stop back," Fargo reminded her.

"She could make you change your mind. I can't risk that," Amber said.

Fargo shrugged. "You've done the deciding, honey. I wouldn't think of arguing with you." He smiled. "Except about one thing." The little frown pushed her brows downward at once. "You'll enjoy," he said.

"I hardly think that," she began, and he cut her off, pulled her to him, and his mouth pressed down over hers. She let him kiss her, kept her lips still, and he smiled inwardly and stepped back. He walked to where his bedroll lay on the soft needles of the forest floor. She followed and he turned to her, slid trousers and shorts off in one quick motion, and stood naked before her, the desire gathering itself at once, his maleness responding, thickening, lengthening, reaching upward.

He watched Amber's eyes fasten on it, stay riveted,

saw her lips part and heard the tiny hiss of breath escape her. He reached for her again, more roughly this time, pulled her to him, and his pulsating organ pushed into the softness of her belly. He pulled at the blouse with both hands and the buttons flew open. Her breasts, softly rounded, pillowy, very white with pale-pink nipples, fell forward, and his hands found their downy softness.

"Oh . . ." she murmured as he closed both hands around them, cupping each, gently lifting and pulling. He released both soft mounds, took her by the waist, and swung her down onto the bedroll.

His mouth found her lips again, his tongue darting forward, opening her lips, and his hands were caressing the pillowy breasts, his thumbs pressing across the small, pale-pink points. She held her lips still for perhaps another half-minute and then he felt her mouth move under his, respond, her tongue come out to meet his darting surrogate organ. He took his mouth from hers after a moment, let his lips trace a simmering path down across her shoulders, over one breast, down to the tiny tip, closing around the softness, sucking, pulling, circling the pink pinnacle with his tongue.

"Oh . . . oooooh . . . oh, no . . . wait . . . aaaah . . ." The cries came suddenly as she stirred under him; his hands pushed down the riding skirt, pulled it loose, his maleness coming down over the warm flesh of her slightly convex little belly. He drew his lips from her breasts, let his fingers gently caress each mound, and gazed down at her loveliness, her long-waisted body a creamy willow wand, flat abdomen and slightly curved little belly, and at the bottom of it, a jet bush, thick and dense and pushed upward by the little mound beneath it.

He drew his fingers slowly through its denseness and saw her long legs draw up, fall back, half-twist. He took one breast in his mouth again and she gasped in pleasure as his fingers moved through the jet bush, slowly dipped to the end of the black triangle. Her moistness surprised him, her skin damp, and he heard her tiny hiss of breath. His fingers found the dark softness, pressed, slowly caressed.

"Oh, oh, oh, my God . . . oh, oh, oh . . . aaaah . . . aaah, no . . . ah, no, please, oh, God." The words came in a single breathless rush, falling against each other, opposites that were not really opposite at all.

Fargo saw her long willow legs stay together as they twisted and he let his hand press between her thighs. The creamy wands parted at once and he felt Amber Holloway's hands dig into his back as he pressed his throbbing maleness against the moist portal, held it there. "Oh, my God. Oh, please . . . please . . . oh, God please," she cried, her voice rising, becoming a half-scream of demand. She was softly wet, flowing around him as he slid upward into the sweet darkness and heard the gasped intake of her breath, a sound of shuddered ecstasy. "Ooooh . . . aaah . . . aaah . . . aaah . . ." she breathed, long sighing sounds in rhythm with his every slow motion inside her.

He felt her hips lift, begin to move with him, no hurried, frantic frenzy for Amber but a slow, sinuous dance of flesh. Her warmth rose with his every motion, her body moving with an almost gentle, swaying rhythm, abdomen sucking in with his every stroke. He pulled back and forth inside her in long, slow strokes, and with each one her gasped breath grew deeper, longer, until her cries were almost one long throaty moan. Suddenly he felt her legs lifting, come around him, pull him deep inside her, and her cry was made of gasped air and then little half-laughing, half-sighing sounds. She quivered against him and he felt her shimmer, close around his throbbing inside her as she pulled him down to lay over her breasts.

"God . . . God," she whispered, a barely audible sound. "Oh, oh, my God." He came with her, burst with her, and her whispered cry became a deep throaty rasp as she tightened legs around him, clung quivering against him until the spiraling ecstasy shattered and she could only cling to the echo in the flesh. She went limp only when that, too, evaporated into warm nothingness. She gave another pleasured shudder when he slowly drew from her to lay half atop her, his eyes enjoying the beauty of her long-waisted body, the soft, cupped turn of her breasts, the smooth indentations of waist that flowed ito rounded hips. Amber Holloway had no hard edges, no saucy, sharply turned places. She was fashioned of soft, slow curves and smooth, willowy beauty. Her closed eyes came open. blinked, focused on the handsome, intense face above her.

"I'd say you enjoyed pretty damn well," Fargo remarked.

A tiny mask of satisfaction slipped over her eyes as she pushed up on her elbows, reached for her blouse. "You made it so. I'll give you that much," she murmured, slipped the blouse on, buttoned it quickly, and reached for her skirt. "But it's done now. I matched her offer," Amber said, slipping the skirt over her long legs.

Fargo drew on shorts, answered without looking at her. "What offer?" he said casually. He glanced up to see Amber's quick flash of eyes as she buttoned the skirt around her waist.

"What do you mean, what offer?" She frowned. "You know very well what offer."

Fargo shrugged, let himself seem confused. "I don't know what you're talking about, honey," he said.

"Jody Tanner's offer," she almost shouted, and the frown grew deeper on her brow.

Fargo continued to look innocently surprised. "I never said she made me an offer," he said blandly.

Amber's voice grew ominous, a tiny tremble creeping into it. "Are you telling me she didn't? She did nothing, promised nothing?" she speared.

"Never said she did," Fargo remarked casually. "You came to that conclusion all by yourself."

The gathering fury inside Amber exploded. A hand shot out, but he pulled his head back and she missed. "You dirty, stinking bastard. You tricked me," she shouted.

Fargo shrugged mildly again. "You tricked yourself. I never said a word," he reminded her.

"Bastard," she screamed again, tried another blow, but this time he caught her hand, spun her away. "You let me believe she'd made you an offer," she said, eyes blazing copper fire. *"Bastard!"*

Fargo smiled pleasantly. "You let yourself believe. Keep the facts straight, honey," he said. "I didn't say a word one way or the other."

"I know what the facts are. The facts are that you're a rotten bastard," Amber stormed, spun on her heel, and strode to her horse.

"You so mad bacause you gave it away for the wrong reasons?" Fargo laughed.

"Bastard," she flung at him again as she pulled herself onto the horse. "Don't stop back next week or ever. I never want to see you again, do you hear me?"

"I hear you," Fargo said.

Amber Holloway shot copper-flame eyes at him from the saddle. "You can scout for Jody Tanner or do whatever you want for her. She doesn't work or ranch or do anything but entertain army officers. That's right, that's all she is. That Lieutenant Richardson took over the post four months ago. Before him there was another officer who visited her place every week. You're welcome to her kind." Amber wheeled the horse, started to race away.

"You still enjoyed," Fargo called after her, listened until the sound of the hoofbeats faded away. He slowly sank down on his bedroll, let a deep sigh escape him as he stretched out. Amber Holloway's fury hadn't been unexpected, only the depth of it. But so had the depth of her passion. It had been a day of surprises and he lay back and let thoughts slowly revolve in his mind, sort themselves into some kind of logic.

Amber Holloway hardly seemed the picture Jody Tanner had painted, a force of ruthless greed directing the massacre of poor settlers. Nor did Jody fit Amber's picture of her as a kind of camp girl, almost an army prostitute. He couldn't buy either—not yet, anyway, not without a lot more proof for either.

The face of Sam Bowdy swam across his thoughts. Had he really made too many enemies? Fargo's lips pulled back in a grimace. That explanation was stretching the long arm of coincidence out of its socket. The man had waited for him, had wanted to tell him

48

something, and had been killed to stop him from doing so. Even his killer hadn't fit the pattern of hired gunmen.

Something was rotten somewhere, rotten and dirty, and he thought of the wagon train and one word hung in front of him . . . "murder." The men, women, and children had been murdered, not simply slain. There would have been an honesty in Cheyenne savage fury, but these were innocent victims, sacrificed for something else, and that made it worse. Somebody deserved to pay, and he felt the anger surge through him and knew he'd follow through to find the truth. The innocent deserved that much.

Amber's round-cheeked face came into his thoughts again. She was consumed with getting her hides to market. Was she consumed enough to commit elaborate murder for her ambitions? Again he had to reject the thought for now. A little beaver bargaining and honest passion was one thing. Ruthlessness was another. Amber would stay a fascinating question mark for now. Jody Tanner came into his thoughts. She was a different kind of fascinating question mark, and he smiled at the thought that drifted across his mind. The possibility waited, certainly worth a try, he mused. The little smile still touched his lips as he fell asleep.

4

He hadn't gone so far as to formulate a plan as he rode through the bur oak and onto the long road. But the thought had hovered in front of him when he woke, gathered his things, and set out, intriguing, captivating, a thought full of delicious possibilities. It stayed as he approached the house that straddled the end of the road, a small frame structure, once white and now a yellowed echo of its former self. Beyond it, where it formed the end of the road, a long field of white-flowered sweet clover stretched in an upward slope. He caught the shine of new-wheat hair as Jody stepped from the house.

Fargo swung from the saddle as she came forward, her misty-blue eyes surveying him with cool questions. "Saw the old man riding upland," Fargo remarked.

"His name's Charles," she said. "He'll be roaming most of the day. He likes to gather things, fruits, berries, chokecherry, pasture brake, whatever he finds."

"He kin of yours?" Fargo asked casually.

"No," she said. "He's just an old drifter, used to work at a ranch a friend owned. My friend closed down and I took Charles on as a handyman. He's good at hard chores despite his age.''

Fargo watched as Jody peered at him, one hand coming to rest on her hip, a loose white shirt lightly touching the very tips of her breasts with surprising provocativeness.

"Seen Amber Holloway?'' she asked, and he nodded. "Going to take her wagons out?'' she pressed.

He half-smiled, chose answers with the same care he had the night before. "That's what brought me here,'' he said.

"You tell her you met me?'' Jody asked, and he nodded again. "That sealed it, didn't it? She made sure you'd agree to take her wagons out. She offered more than the money, I'll bet.'' Fargo allowed a half-shrug. "Now you've come back to see what I'll offer,'' Jody announced with a kind of bitchy smugness coming into her face.

"You asking or offering?'' he said, and heard the echo in the question.

Jody Tanner's mist-blue eyes darkened. "Damn, Fargo, you ought to want to find out the truth about all this,'' she flared.

"Why? I've my own roads to follow. I don't need any more,'' he said.

"Because it's the right thing to do,'' she threw back. "I oughtn't to have to offer anything.''

"You don't have to,'' he said mildly, and started to turn back to the pinto.

"Wait,'' she said quickly, and he paused. "If I'm offering, what will it mean?'' she questioned with a sullen frown. "You won't go back and take her wagons through. You'll find out about her and those fake Cheyenne raids," Jody said.

"Fair enough," he agreed, and watched the tiny glimmer of triumph touch the mist-blue eyes. He waited and saw her lips tighten as she suddenly wrestled with inner conflicts. Finally she turned, almost growled words at him.

"Come inside," she said, and he followed her into a small living room, sparsely furnished, a few chairs, a worn sofa, and a wooden cabinet. She stepped into an adjoining room, a bedroom, he saw, and equally sparsely furnished, a weathered dresser the only piece in the room other than the wide bed. The house had a transient feeling about it and he thought of how Amber had characterized Jody as being an army camp follower. He frowned inwardly as he watched Jody start to pull her shirt from the waistband of her skirt and he saw the tight, tense lines that had come to touch her face. They struck down Amber's words. No camp girl, he grunted silently. Camp girls didn't grow tense at moments such as this. No camp girl, he repeated, but she was certainly consumed with an inner drive. They both were, he reflected: Amber willing to give her all to get her hides safely to market, consumed with her own goals; and Jody willing to do the same for rage and vengeance. It'd be a waste to let all that consuming intensity go to waste. He smiled inwardly, began to take off his clothes.

He paused to watch Jody slowly, almost hesitantly, toy with the buttons of her shirt. "Relax," he said. "You're supposed to enjoy yourself."

"You do the enjoying," she snapped.

He shook his head. "No, no, sweetie. I don't dance by myself," he said. He reached out, took her hand

52

from the button, slowly undid the button for her. He undid the next one as his eyes held her mist-blue orbs in a steady gaze. His hand moved down, undoing the rest of the buttons, and the blouse came open.

"No, wait," she began to protest, but his hand reached forward, cupped itself around one soft-firm breast, and he heard her breath draw in sharply. His mouth closed over hers and he let his tongue move across the inside of her lips. He felt her hands tighten against him, her mouth open, and her tongue slip forward in a hesitant answer. He pushed the shirt from her, stepped back, took a moment to gaze at her. No soft pillowy breasts for Jody Tanner, he saw, but two firmly curved mounds, on the small side, but beautifully formed, with little cherry-red nipples that pointed upward. His hands pushed her skirt down slowly and he watched a slightly curved abdomen appear, then a convex little belly as the skirt fell to her ankles and she stood beautifully naked before him, hips wide and flat and full thighs that tapered to nice-enough legs. His gaze lingered at the light-brown, almost-blond little triangle. A shudder went through her and he felt her hands grasp his shoulders, start to push back, but he dropped to one knee and pressed his face into the small, firm breasts, took one cherry-red nipple into his mouth.

"Aaaaah," she gasped as he slowly circled his tongue around the nipple. "Oh . . . oh, God." He pressed her back onto the bed, drew back from her, and stood straight as he finished slipping his trousers off. He saw the mist-blue eyes grow even more misted as she looked at the powerful, thrusting, reaching maleness of him, pulsating with erect desire. Again a shudder went through

53

her and he saw her lips part, heard tiny gasped sounds come from them.

He moved down to the bed, rested his body half over hers, let his hardness press against the blond nap and his hands slowly move down the softness of her, skin lightly tanned and smooth to the touch; and again he drew the upturned breasts into his mouth, moving from one to the other, taking his time, pulling gently, kissing, sucking the little cherry-red tips into his mouth.

"Oh, oh, oh, God . . . oh, my God," Jody breathed, and he felt her body begin to move, twist one way, then the other, her legs moving with it. His hand traced a tantalizing pathway down across the very center of her torso, down over the little belly, and her abdomen sucked in with reaction, came forward again, and he felt her legs move apart, quickly close again. His hand pushed down through the blond bush, rested for a moment on the soft mound underneath, pressed harder, and he let one finger find the warm, dark place just beneath.

"Aaaaeeeiiii . . ." she half-screamed once, then again. He caressed and the scream became a groan. Gently, slowly, he let his hand close over the portal of portals, held there, cupping the entrance. "Oh, oh, God," Jody cried out, and her torso lifted with the desire born of the flesh, beyond commanding, beyond obeying anything but itself. He pressed deeper with his hand, pressed the cup harder against her, and then let his fingers move in, explore, and her legs opened, her hips twisting and moving upward. He touched deeply, caressed, stroked the softness, and she was making little moaning noises in between words. "Oh God . . . ah . . . ah, yes . . . no . . . ah, ah, Jesus," she murmured.

He lifted himself, came over her, and pressed his hot,

throbbing maleness against the dense blond mound. Again Jody Tanner screamed, and he felt her body tensing, stiffening. He moved into her quickly, then thrust slowly, then faster. Little garbled sounds fell from her lips and he saw the new-wheat hair tossing from one side to the other in frenzy, a shimmering shower of gold flashes. He matched the frenzied tossing of her hair with his thrusts and buried his mouth into the firm, upturned breasts.

"Yes, yes . . . please, oh, please, please," Jody screamed into his ear. He slowed, drew half away from her. "No . . . God, no," she screamed, and then groaned as he plunged forward. He felt her body grow suddenly taut and her fingers dug into the bedsheet. "Ah . . . ah . . . ah . . ." she breathed, the gathering ecstasy pushing every sound from her. He held, then plunged as she exploded under him and her blond nap pushed up with a kind of desperate fury of ecstasy, hitting against his pelvis, little sharp thrusts, that continued through that hanging moment, kept on until there was nothing left but the quivering remains of passion consumed, turned in on itself.

He lay beside her, on one elbow, enjoyed the loveliness of the lightly tanned body, the cherry-red tips that asked to be caressed. Slowly her eyes came open, the mist-blue veiled, finally focusing through the curtain. Her hand moved, touched his chest, traced down to his abdomen with one finger.

"You read more than the wind," Jody murmured. "It's more than experience. It's a special kind of awareness."

"Trail or tail, you have to know what to look for," Fargo said.

Jody pushed herself up to a sitting position, the firm little mounds standing upward with their own pert beauty. "When are you going to tell Amber Holloway you won't be taking her wagons out?" she asked.

"Don't have to," Fargo said blandly. His quick glance saw the frown appear on Jody's forehead.

"What do you mean?" she asked.

"Her teams went lame. She won't be ready for at least a week, maybe two," Fargo remarked casually.

He saw the frown spread and Jody's lips moved before the words came. "You bastard," she hissed, pulling herself up straighter. "You lied to me."

"Try again, honey," Fargo said mildly.

"You tricked me," she threw back.

Fargo smiled inwardly. Echoes, variations, different melody, same words, he grunted to himself.

"I didn't have to offer anything to stop you from taking her wagons out, damn you," Jody accused. "I never had to match her offer."

"Never said you did," Fargo remarked as he slipped into trousers.

"You let me jump to conclusions," she returned.

He shrugged as he finished dressing. "You did the jumping, honey," he said. "Before and after."

"Don't add crudeness to it," she snapped.

"Truth, Jody, honey, just truth." He laughed.

"Dammit, Fargo, you find out what I want to know. You owe me that now," she flung back.

Fargo felt the anger snap to the surface. Amber had been merely infuriated. There was a self-righteousness to Jody's anger than irritated him.

"You not owed a damn thing," he snapped. "You outsmarted yourself. If there's any owing due here, it's to the innocent who've been murdered." He turned, finished dressing, and strapped on his gun belt as he headed for the door.

"Fargo," she called, and the selfishness was gone from her tone, replaced by a note of desperation. "Are you going to look? Will you find out?" she asked.

He paused at the door. "Maybe," he grunted. "If I do, it won't be for you."

"When will I know?" she asked.

"When I tell you," he said curtly.

"Wait," she cried as he started out. "Where can I find you?"

"I'll do the finding for now," he tossed back as he walked from the house. He glimpsed the new-wheat hair at a window as he rode away. He headed upland, feeling satisfied and not at all guilty. Two young women had learned that pussy-waving could backfire. They owed him a vote of thanks for that lesson. Not that they'd be giving him that, but they'd remember, he was certain. More than the lesson, he smiled as he crossed a slope; he kept moving upward to a high plateau where he found a fast-running brook and halted, dismounted to let the pinto drink. He took his canteen and started to fill it when he caught the sound of hoofbeats on the other side of a small rise.

Fargo's hand was on the butt of the big Colt .45 at once, his body instantly taut. In seconds, he relaxed, his hand moving from the gun. No Cheyenne, he grunted, the cadenced hoofbeats of horses being ridden side by side, in a column of twos. He had just put the cap on his canteen when Lieutenant Richardson and his troop came into view. He saw the lieutenant spot him in surprise, move his platoon down to the brook. The lieutenant's young face was still made of youthful arrogance and army stiffness.

"Looking for Cheyenne?" Fargo asked blandly.

"Cheyenne, wagon trains, either one," the lieutenant clipped out. "I stopped at Jody Tanner's place yesterday. You certainly convinced her the wagon-train attacks weren't the Cheyenne."

"Her, but not you." Fargo smiled.

"Absolutely not me," Lt. Richardson said with disdain. "All of it really contrived reasoning. Perhaps you enjoy impressing the inexperienced."

"I enjoy seeing what others don't see," Fargo said.

The lieutenant made a wry sound. "You enjoy making up stories," he said. "It's the Cheyenne. My troop has seen them trailing wagon trains. They ran when they saw us coming after them."

"Be glad they ran," Fargo grunted.

"It would seem they have a greater respect for this troop's fighting abilities than you do," the lieutenant snapped.

Fargo's eyes stayed mild. "It would seem so," he agreed.

The lieutenant's lips tightened as he raised his arm into the air, brought it down sharply, and led the platoon off in a trot. Fargo watched the column move away. The lieutenant had his young troopers ride smartly, as though they were on parade.

Fargo shook his head as he turned away, fastened his canteen in place, and swung up onto the pinto to slowly continue his path upland. He rode slowly, halted on high ground, and let his gaze travel in a slow half-circle as he scanned the land below. Lush land, mostly wooded, but he saw three flat places, three natural avenues for a wagon rolling westward to the immediate area or going on farther. Even a tenderfoot could keep them in view, he muttered to himself, and he moved downward, found another place that commanded a view of the three flat paths and afforded a good cover of red oak. He stayed, his eyes taking in the surrounding land, and he found six more places that offered a view of the three flat avenues below and held good cover. Six, dammit, he swore under his breath, too many to cover.

He moved on, continued downward to lower land, threaded his way between a sudden outcrop of shale. A cluster of rotten logs covered with elf's-cap moss lay near the shale, and he let the pinto jump easily across the obstacles. He emerged from behind the outcrop of shale and halted. The old man rode along a ridgeline not too far way, and Fargo watched. Charles moved his horse slowly, in a deliberate pattern, his eyes on the ground below where the three flat pathways almost paralleled one another. He seemed to do more looking than gathering, Fargo mused, though he carried a bundle of chokecherry across the saddle in front of him. Fargo moved the pinto forward to cross in front of the old man, nodded as he came to a halt.

"I hear your name's Charles," Fargo remarked.

"It is," the old man said.

"Just Charles?" Fargo asked.

"One name is enough for most people, I've always felt," he answered.

Fargo let a smile mask the sharpness of his eyes. No old drifter, no old handyman, Fargo murmured silently. The old man spoke with the diction of an educated man, his hands uncalloused, hands that roped no steers, wielded no tools.

"Been with Jody long?" Fargo asked casually.

Charles gave a half-shrug. "Everything seems long when you grow old," he said. "A good day to you, sir."

Fargo nodded in return, watched the old man move his horse on, and he let the frown come to his brow only when Charles had disappeared over the ridge. No old drifter, he muttered again. Turn-away answers that revealed nothing, Fargo murmured, polite, agreeable, yet turn-away answers. But by their very caution they had said something. They'd said that Jody's story about Charles, if that were really his name, had been made-to-order and agreed upon by both of them. There could be a thousand explanations, and he decided to put aside speculation. But little Jody had another lesson to learn. Spotting a wrong trail was part of being a trailsman.

Fargo rode on and his eyes swept back and forth across the ground as he rode. He smiled grimly as he came upon the signs, the little signs few men would see and fewer still would understand. The forest floor was covered with a thick growth of soft grass that revealed no hoofprints as such, but he saw the blades of grass pressed down in regular, oval shapes, and he dismounted, examined the grass closely. No broken edges around the oval shapes that horseshoes would have caused. Unshod Indian ponies, he grunted, and went on. He spotted the slain owl soon after, the talons carefully removed for a necklace. The Cheyenne, he reckoned grimly, the real ones. The trail was fresh, and he followed it farther, saw the trail move out of the woodland onto a hill, where the hoofprints became clear. Six, he counted; he reined up as another set of hoofprints joined the first. Ten in the second band, perhaps twelve, he counted.

The two Cheyenne bands joined together and headed northwest.

Fargo followed again, finally halted as he saw the day beginning to ebb. The Cheyenne had been riding leisurely and steadily, no sudden forays to scout. They were on their way back to a camp, not too far away, he surmised. Fargo turned and retraced steps, made his way back toward the stand of balsams where he'd camped the night before. He'd started up a slow rise when the band of horsemen appeared to his left and the big Colt was in his hand instantly. He returned the gun to its holster when he recognized Ken Dixon at the head of the riders. He halted as Dixon and his men rode up to him.

"Everybody's out on the countryside today," Fargo remarked.

"Six calves got out. We've been looking for them," Ken Dixon said.

"This far from the ranch?" Fargo asked with some surprise.

"Don't know how long they've been out. We're playing it safe," Dixon said.

"How are the horses?" Fargo asked.

"Just what Amber asked me this morning," the ranch foreman said. "They're still lame. I'm using oil of wintergreen now."

"She say anything else?" Fargo queried.

"Nope," Dixon said, and Fargo held the small smile inside himself. "Be seeing you, Fargo," Dixon said, and moved his men on.

Fargo slowly continued on his way and reached the balsams as night touched the land. He made a fire of a handful of twigs, just enough to warm some beef jerky, ate leisurely, and relaxed on his bedroll when he finished. The night sky a black carpet studded with jewels, he kept thoughts pushed back in the recesses of his mind, listened to the night sounds.

He hadn't waited long when the sound of the horse drifted up the slope, slow, soft hoofbeats, a lone rider moving carefully but with no effort to be stealthy.

He stayed relaxed, stretched out on the bedroll, but caution was too ingrained a part of him to discard entirely, and his hand moved to rest against the butt of the Colt. He watched the night move, shadows part, take on form, and the rider come into the dim glow of the fire's embers, brown hair hanging loosely around an oval face, amber eyes just catching the tiniest flicker of firelight.

Amber Holloway swung to the ground, her long-waisted form a graceful line, the curve of one thigh pressing against a close-fitting skirt. She looked down at the big man, followed him with her eyes as he rose to sit up, her face set.

"Dammit, Fargo, you might have the decency to look surprised," she snapped.

"Why? I'm not," he said.

"That's what I call being conceited," Amber returned.

"It's what I call being observant. I met your foreman. You didn't tell him you'd sent me packing. I figured there had to be a reason." Fargo smiled.

She hesitated, searched for a quick reply. "Maybe it just slipped my mind," she said.

Fargo laughed. "That's not even a good grade of bullshit, honey," he said.

She glowered back, her full, red lower lip thrust forward almost in a pout, and he remembered the soft

warmth of her lips. "All right, it didn't slip my mind,"
Amber conceded. He saw her eyes narrow as she pushed
the next question at him. "You see Jody Tanner already?"
she asked.

"I saw her." He nodded.

"You working for her now?" Amber pressed.

"No," he said, the answer true enough. "But you
didn't come all the way up here just to ask me that," he
said.

"No," she conceded.

"Good," he said, and saw her eyes flare at his smile.

"And it's not what you're thinking," she snapped at
once.

He let mock dismay touch his face. "Well, then,
why'd you come?" he asked.

"I came because I need you, Fargo. I need you for
all the reasons I sent for you in the first place. I realized
that after I cooled down. Getting my wagons through
safely is more important to me than anything else. I
spent all night thinking about that," she said.

"Just that?" Fargo smiled.

Her lips tightened. "No, not just that," she admitted.
"But there won't be any more of the other."

"What other?" he pushed.

Her lips pressed tight again. "Beaver bargaining, I
believe you called it," she said icily.

"I believe I did," Fargo agreed. "I'm glad to hear
that."

Her lips parted in surprise, the tiny frown touching
his brow. "You are?" she asked, and he nodded. "I
confess surprise at that," she said.

"Now you can do it for the right reasons." He
smiled.

"I didn't say I'd do it for any reason," she snapped.

"No, I just did," he answered affably.

Her eyes glowed a soft yellow. "Dammit, Fargo, I came to ask you to help me, to stick to our agreement and wait till the horses are ready, just a little longer. Forget about working for Jody Tanner. It won't be a long wait. Pay, no pay, whatever you want, but just wait and take me through," she said, swallowed hard. "This is as close as I've ever come to begging anybody to do anything."

He saw the pain touch her eyes. "I imagine that's true enough," he commented, looked past her into the night as he ruffled thoughts through his mind. He wanted questions answered. This was as good a way as any to start, and he returned his gaze to her, saw the apprehension in her face as she watched him. "I want to know more," he said.

"About what?" she asked.

"Amber Holloway, for starters," he answered.

"What difference does that make?" She frowned.

"It might decide whether you're worth helping or not," he said. "You said there were a lot of people waiting to see you fail. Would your daddy be one of them?"

Her chin lifted, her face growing tight. "Yes," she said almost angrily. "He and Jeff Stuart."

"Who's that?"

"The man Daddy wanted me to marry, all hand-picked and passed inspection," Amber said, the bitterness coming into her voice at once. "That's what he wanted for me, to stay home and marry and spend my time giving fancy lawn parties at the mansion."

"You've other ideas," Fargo injected.

"Always had. That's not for me. Daddy and I had a terrible fight when I told him I wasn't staying or marrying Jeff Stuart. I'd a little money of my own, enough to start this place. He was furious with me, hasn't written to me since I left. Daddy's an old-fashioned southern gentleman. He doesn't believe in girls going out on their own."

"Maybe he's not as mad as you think," Fargo said.

Her laugh was hard. "He's mad enough to disown me. Nobody crosses Colonel Hudson Holloway the way I did. He's a powerful man back home in Virginia. He controls most people around him and our plantation is practically the state's second capital."

"But he softened enough to give you Ken Dixon," Fargo pointed out.

Amber frowned into space. "You know, that's something I've never been able to figure out. It's not him. It's just not my daddy. Colonel Hudson Holloway doesn't soften and doesn't forgive. People that cross him find that he still has them in his grip. He's the most ruthlessly determined man I've ever known."

The thought flared in Fargo's mind. Like father, like daughter? But he let it stay unvoiced and commented instead, "Your Virginia accent gets stronger when you get excited," he said.

"I've been told that before." She half-smiled.

"So all this is to prove yourself to Daddy?" he asked.

"And to myself. I've got to see if what I've done is as great as I think it is. If I'm going to be an independent woman I've got to see if I can cut it," she answered.

"And nothing much else matters but that," Fargo slid out.

"Not much else," she agreed coolly.

"You've a real thing about Jody Tanner. Why?" he asked.

Again Amber thought for a moment before replying. "Disliked her from the first time we met. Personality clash, I guess. Then she began to say things about my claiming so much land and started calling me names."

"Such as?"

"Greedy. Uncaring. Selfish. She accused me of using my money to freeze poor settlers out of land. I outbid a friend of hers for the north forty and she's held that against me ever since," Amber said with disdain in her voice. "But then I know what she is, just Yankee trash," she added.

"Now who's calling names?" Fargo said.

Amber let her face soften. "You're right. I shouldn't stoop to her level," she said. "Any more questions?"

He gazed past her into the night. "I guess not," he murmured, and lapsed into thought.

Her impatience refused to let her wait more than a half-minute. "Well?" he heard her ask, brought his eyes back to her.

"See me when you're ready to roll," he said.

"That's not much of a yes," she protested.

"It'll do," he said coldly.

"You on the payroll?" she asked.

"Not till those wagons roll," he answered.

She stepped closer, her full, red lower lip thrust forward, almost that little-girl pout again. "Thanks," she said, and made the word sound tentative. She was a package of sudden contrasts, consuming determination and vulnerable openness, appealing warmth and waspish bitchiness.

He leaned forward, pressed his mouth on hers, and she started to push away, halted, stayed, and he felt her lips part. He drew away. It wasn't the moment for anything more.

"What was that for?" she said, almost glowing.

"For yesterday and tomorrow, a reminder and a promise." He laughed.

"I don't need either," she returned stiffly, and pulled herself onto her horse. She looked down at him coolly. "You going to camp here regularly?" she asked.

"For now." He grinned. "So's you can find me in case you get any sudden urges," he said.

The amber eyes flashed. "I won't be," she snapped, and sent the horse into a canter.

His laugh followed her into the dark and he found himself thinking of the flowing sinuousness of her lovemaking, the creamy willow body and pillowed breasts. There'd be another time. Soon, he told himself. He'd see to that, before he came onto truths that might make him turn away.

"Truths." The word hung before him. How many truths had Amber given him? Her feelings about her pa had been real, words too angry for acting, and she'd admitted to the heredity for determination and ruthlessness. She had seemed to talk openly, and yet, as he thought about it, she hadn't really told him anything that mattered. Yet the cold-blooded murdering of settlers, the elaborate deception of faking Cheyenne raids, it was all too vicious for ambition, even ruthless ambition. There had to be more behind it, something deeper and darker that plunged into the soul far stronger than the determination to prove oneself. The stakes had to be bigger than that. And Amber had to remain a question mark. Not because of Jody's accusations but because of Sam Bowdy, killed for what he wanted to tell, and because of a killer who took his own life rather than risk being forced to talk. Fargo's lips tightened. More than just a girl's ambition, he muttered again.

He undressed slowly, wrapped himself in his bedroll, and let sleep push away his thoughts. Whatever the truth, it remained as dark and cloaked as the night. He'd have to find a tear in the cloak. Or make one. He turned on his side and slept, one hand resting lightly on the grip of the big Colt.

5

Fargo wiped tiny beads of perspiration from his brow. The sun had been hot when he woke and had grown hotter as the morning lengthened and he rode the flat avenue of grass. He'd seen no signs of wagon trains, only a distant horseman riding hard, and he turned the pinto to start back the way he'd come. He paused to watch a ridge where a troop flag suddenly appeared, followed by Lt. Richardson and his platoon.

Fargo moved on as the sun reached the noon sky, turned the pinto down the second flat stretch of soft Spanish clover, and rode leisurely eastward. He finally turned when he found no signs of oncoming wagon trains and once more made his way back, climbed up to one of the vantage points he had marked out, and let his eyes sweep the horizon. He spotted only the thin spiral of dust that marked the cavalry troop still scouting the distant ridges for sign of the Cheyenne.

Fargo waited at the vantage place, scanned the terrain in slow circles, and stayed until he saw the sun begin to slip down behind the hills and the day start to grow dim. He started down from the place and then up the long slope that led to the stand of balsams.

He'd gone halfway up the incline when the six riders appeared from a line of bur oak and he recognized Ken Dixon at the head. The ranch foreman saw the Ovaro and turned toward the horse. Fargo halted, let the riders rein up before him. Ken Dixon's sandy hair pushed out from beneath his tan hat, his strong jaw set tight, his eyes in a frowning, piercing stare.

"Been hearing things about you, Fargo," Dixon said with an edge in his voice.

"Like what?" Fargo asked mildly.

"It seems you don't think it's Cheyenne that have been hitting the wagon trains," the man said, the frown in his voice.

Fargo smiled. "Where'd you hear that?" he asked evenly.

"Some of my men went into Hollowville last night. They got to talking with a half-dozen soldier boys at the dance hall. The soldier boys told them what you'd said to the lieutenant," Dixon answered.

Fargo kept his smile as he swore silently. Of course, the troopers would have heard his exchange with Richardson. He hadn't thought about saloon talk, and he swore again at himself.

"You really believe what you told the lieutenant?" Dixon said, breaking into his thoughts.

"That's right." Fargo nodded. "I get the feeling you don't agree."

"Damn right. That's crazy talk if I ever heard it, Fargo. It's the damn Cheyenne. Who in hell else would it be?" Ken Dixon barked.

"Don't have answers for that," Fargo said.

"Then going around with that kind of talk can get you in trouble, Fargo," Ken Dixon said.

"Why?" Fargo asked, keeping his voice bland.

"Hell, if it ain't the Cheyenne, you're as good as accusing somebody around here. Folks won't take kindly to that, I can tell you," the ranch foreman said, anger thickening his Virginia accent as it did with Amber. "And you can be sure that others have heard about it by now," he added.

"No doubt." Fargo sighed. "But I didn't accuse anyone."

"But it's not the Cheyenne, you stick to that?" the man pressed.

"That's right," Fargo answered.

Ken Dixon's face grew contemptuous with disbelief. "Speaking plain, Fargo, if this is a sample of how you read things, I don't know that you ought to be taking the wagons through," he said.

Fargo managed a tight smile. "One vote of no confidence, is that it?" he said. "I'd guess that's for Amber to decide."

"It is, but I'll speak my piece to her," the foreman said protectively, and wheeled his horse away as the others followed.

Fargo stayed motionless, let the men go out of sight before slowly moving on. Damn, he swore silently. He hadn't wanted his thoughts spread beyond Jody and the lieutenant, not till he'd had more time to watch, wait, find a lead. But that had been blown away now and again he cursed loose-tongued soldiers and their saloon talk.

The irritation stayed with him as he reached the balsams, moved through the back of the forest to his camping spot, and he pondered Ken Dixon's reactions. They had matched Lt. Richardson's in disbelief and rejection. Richardson's attitude was made of conceit and inexperience. Was Ken Dixon's fashioned out of the same cloth, or something more? He pondered the question, added it to the fast-growing list of unanswered ones.

Night came before he made the campsite. He unsaddled, laid out his bedroll, and nibbled on some beef jerky. He decided to make a small fire, just large enough to brew fresh coffee. He had the old, enameled pot over the flames, the coffee brewing, when he heard a horse moving fast up the slope. He rose, peered into the silvered dimness, and saw the rider approaching, caught the trail of long hair blown in the wind. He stepped back into the trees and returned to the fire.

He was draining the coffee grounds as the horse reached the camp, and he watched Amber swing down from the saddle, her face tight. "Coffee?" he asked as he held a tin cup out to her. She nodded and took the cup, moved to a tree, and sank down with her back against it. He folded himself in front of her and watched her take a long pull of the hot brew, her eyes finding him with a frown.

"You expect me again?" she asked almost petulantly.

"No, not this time," he said honestly.

"But you know why I'm here," she probed.

He gave a half-shrug. "I can guess. Ken Dixon said his piece to you."

She nodded, sipped the coffee. "He did," she murmured.

Fargo laughed softly. "And you're wondering if he's right," he said.

She continued to stare gravely at him. "I have to wonder," she said. "You must have reasons for what you've said."

"I do." Fargo smiled.

"Ken said they'd be as crazy as your ideas," Amber told him.

"And what do you say?" Fargo asked.

"I came to hear," she answered.

Fargo let his lips purse in thought for a moment. "Fair enough," he answered, and proceeded to detail his reasons for deciding it was no Cheyenne attack. He omitted mention of Jody Tanner and let her think he'd given the reasons to the lieutenant. He let a smile touch his face when he finished, an edge of wryness in it.

"Now you have a problem," he said. She frowned in question. "You've got to decide whether to believe me or the others," he finished.

Amber finished her coffee and put the cup down, turned her eyes on him, round and deepened with concern. "I want to believe you, but what that means makes me feel sick inside," she said. "Someone deliberately massacring wagon trains and posing as the Cheyenne. Who and why? It's just too horrible."

"You've lived here a year. Got any ideas?" Fargo asked with deceptive casualness as his eyes stayed fastened on Amber Holloway, watching for the tiniest sign in her face, a flicker of carefulness, an instant of caution before answering. But there was nothing, her reply quick.

"No, God, no, none at all. I can't even think of anyone doing it," Amber said. Her hand reached out, closed over his sinewy forearm. "I believe you even if Ken doesn't. I believe you and I hate what that means."

73

Fargo saw her shudder and her hand tightened on his arm. He drew her forward and she came without resistance, leaning into his chest, and he felt the softness of her breasts against him.

"Just hold me for a moment," she breathed, and shuddered again.

He let one hand move up to cup the underside of one breast. "Just hold you?" he asked.

Her reply came on whispered breath. "Yes, just hold me," she said, but made no move to push away from the hand cupping her breast.

He let his thumb lift, move delicately over the front of her breast, soft pressure against the little tip, moved it back again, and heard the tiny gasp from her. He caressed the little point again and felt it rise under the cotton blouse.

"No," she breathed, but he felt her press forward against him. His finger found a button, flipped it open, did the same with another, and warm skin came into his hand. His thumb touched the pink nib, and Amber's breath exhaled in a long sigh. She slid backward, the blouse coming open entirely, and he went with her, his face pressing into the downy softness of the two breasts that closed around him.

"Oh, my God," Amber said, the words drawled, and Fargo kept his mouth moving across her breasts as he pulled off clothes, saw her wriggle free of blouse and skirt, and the warm softness of her against him sent an inflaming spiral of wanting through him. His mouth pulled on one breast, then the other, and he felt her hands moving down over his back, across his nakedness, traveling back up his body in wildly fluttering motions.

"I didn't . . . I didn't come for this," he heard her whisper.

He paused, answered as he held his lips touching one pale-pink tip. "You telling me or yourself," he breathed, pressed his tongue down onto the firm little nob.

"I don't know," she gasped. "I don't know." But her hand came up behind the back of his neck, pulled his mouth over the pillowy breast. He felt her torso begin to move, that slow, undulating, sinuous movement, the soft-wire triangle lifting to push against him. "Ah, ah, ah, God," she suddenly half-screamed as he let his maleness probe, seek, touch the outer lips, take in the warmth of her, then slide forward into the sweet darkness. He moved with the motion of her hips as they lifted and glided at the same time, drew up, then forward and down, up again, forward and down again, the supple, long-waisted body a flowing river of flesh. Tiny drawn-out sounds, almost breathless sounds, escaped her lips with each motion of her torso, and her hands pressed into his back, drawing him to her. Once again he was aware of the sinuous, serpentine flow of her lovemaking, every movement part of an unbroken rhythm that might have been languorous except for the consuming passion of every motion, every gasped cry.

"Fargo," she whispered almost inaudibly. "Faaaaar-go . . . yes, oh, my God, yes." The whispered sounds came, not stronger, but with an added urgency. He felt her stomach suck way in suddenly, thrust upward at once as though she were expelling a deep part of her very essence. She rose up with him, cried out, her mouth against his chest, the slow, languorous flow of her lovemaking becoming a thing of deep, rasped groans, a culmination of desire that welled up as though it were a torrent rushing forth, overflowing, uncontrolled now, consuming and consumed all at once. Her pelvis stayed thrust hard against him as she groaned, her nails pressing into his back, and he lifted her to that final ecstasy as he surged in release with her.

"Aaaaggghhh . . . ah, ah . . . oooh." The sounds tore from her as she tried to cling to the moment that refused all clinging, the spiral that led everywhere and nowhere. He stayed with her as she slid backward, her torso falling to the ground as the final groan left her lips, almost a half-sob echoed by her arms, which clung to him.

He let her lie still until she finally opened her eyes to focus on him. Slowly she shook her head. "I don't believe myself," she said. "I don't believe I let this happen."

"For the right reasons, this time." He smiled and she stared silently back. "Because you wanted to," he finished.

She pushed herself up on her elbows and frowned into space. "I guess so," she murmured, more to herself than to him.

He let his face rest against the side of one pillowy, creamy breast. "What about your wagons?" he asked softly.

"I want you to take them through," she said.

"Even if your foreman thinks I read things all wrong?" he asked.

"I don't care what Ken thinks. He was bothered at my writing to you to come here. A slight case of jealousy, I expect," Amber said.

"Likely," Fargo remarked, pulled himself up onto one elbow. "You get your calves back?" he asked.

"Calves back?" Amber frowned.

"The ones that ran off yesterday," Fargo said as he felt caution stabbing at him.

76

Amber's frown stayed. "First I heard of it," she said.

"Dixon told me. I'd have thought you'd be the first to know," Fargo said.

Amber gave a little half-shrug. "I guess Ken just took off after them in too much of a hurry to tell me," she said.

"Guess so," Fargo agreed mildly, leaned forward, circled one pale-pink nipple with his tongue. "You going to stay the night?" he murmured.

She moved back, reached for her shirt. "And become the gossip of every cowhand's tongue, come morning?" she snapped. "You know better."

Fargo shrugged, pulled on trousers as she put her skirt on. She halted, came to him, and suddenly her amber eyes held a mischievous twinkle. "Tell you what, you just stay here and I might ride this way, come dawn," she said, and pressed herself to him as she buttoned the last button. Her eyes held the twinkle. "What's it like, in the morning?" she half-whispered.

"Better than flapjacks," he told her, and she gave a little-girl giggle, turned, and strode to her horse.

He went with her, let his hand steal under her skirt to caress her thigh as she leaned from the saddle to brush his lips with hers. He watched her ride down the slope until she was out of sight, and he stepped back, his eyes growing narrow in thought. Had Ken Dixon lied about the calves? Had it been a fast answer to explain he and his men roaming the land that far from the ranch? Dixon was good with quick, glib replies, Fargo mused, pondering the man's answers about Sam Bowdy. Amber's surprise at the question of the calves had been genuine, too instant for anything else. The fact was that, up to

77

now, Amber's actions and reactions had been the most straightforward and direct, far more instant and open than Dixon's. Or Jody Tanner's. Fargo frowned as he thought about Jody's story explaining Charles. She had pointed the finger at Amber, yet so far she'd been the one spooning out lies to him. The fact dug at him, irritated, and he pulled on shirt and gun belt. Dixon would bear more attention, Fargo muttered, but meanwhile he'd put an end to Jody's handing him hogwash explanations.

He swung onto the pinto and headed the horse through the balsams and finally out onto a clear slope where a half-moon lighted his way. He moved downward until he reached the roadway beyond the bur oaks, slowed the pinto as the dark bulk of the house came into view, a light on in one window. He slowed, turned the pinto into the trees lining the road, and felt the frown push at his brows. A horse stood tied to the hitching post outside the door, a brown gelding with his lines immediately marking him as a Morgan, the standard U.S. cavalry mount. Moving closer to the house, Fargo made out the U.S. army insignia on the lower-left corner of the saddle skirt. He dismounted, moved through the trees on foot.

Jody was entertaining the military. Amber's remarks about her flew through his mind with their own malicious glee before he could shake them away. He dropped to one knee at the edge of the trees as figures passed by the window inside the house and he saw the front door open. The lieutenant came out, Jody following, clothed in a long dark-blue robe over a nightdress. The wedge of light from the open doorway made a pathway to the lieutenant's mount, where he halted before swinging into the saddle. Fargo saw him turn to Jody, his face arrogantly angry.

"Damn, what makes you believe this Fargo so damn much?" he asked her. "I still say it's the Cheyenne."

"Frankly I believe him because he sees more with his eyes shut than you do with your eyes open," Fargo heard Jody snap back.

"That's a rotten thing to say," Lt. Richardson answered, hurt coming into his angry tone.

"Maybe it is, but being stubborn is stupid. The man is the Trailsman. Reading signs is his life," Jody flung back. "I say he's right, and you just think about what that means. Just think about it."

Fargo watched the lieutenant's face tighten. "I know what it would mean. It'd mean they know," he said.

"Exactly. They know it's on its way and the cover is a wagon or a wagon train," Jody said, and Fargo felt the frown sliding over his forehead as he listened. "Of course they can't go around attacking wagon trains openly. They know we'd realize what that would say. So they've been faking the attacks as the Cheyenne. Had us damn well fooled, too, until Fargo came by. Don't you see how it all fits perfectly?"

Fargo saw the lieutenant grimace. "Dammit, I can see that it fits. I just don't believe it's not the Cheyenne," he shot back, frowned in thought for another moment. "You say you pointed Fargo at Amber Holloway."

"Yes. I'm sure it's her. She fits, too. They all fit down there," Jody said.

"What'd you tell him?" Fargo heard Richardson ask. "Not the truth of it, did you?"

"You take me for a fool? I couldn't risk that. I told him how she was the kind who'd do anything to keep

79

newcomers from settling here," Jody snapped. "I threw in a brother killed in one of the attacks."

Fargo felt the words form on his lips in silent fury. Goddamn, he swore. The lying little bitch. The stinking, little liar. He heard Richardson's voice cut into his thoughts.

"He buy that?" the lieutenant asked.

"Not altogether, but enough to look some on his own," Jody said.

"And you figure he'll bring you proof," Richardson said.

"Would you move your troopers against her without proof?" Jody returned.

"You know I couldn't do that," Fargo heard Richardson say stiffly.

"So Fargo will get it. I'm sure he will," Jody answered.

Richardson swung onto his mount. "We'll see," the lieutenant answered. "Meanwhile, I'll keep patrolling for the Cheyenne until you've something more to give me."

Fargo stayed motionless, watched Richardson canter down the road. His eyes turned to Jody as she returned to the house. She pulled the door closed after her and the wedge of light vanished. Fargo's eyes went to the window and saw Jody come into view, halt beside a table. Charles appeared, the old man clothed in a blue silk dressing robe no drifter would ever see unless he'd stolen it. Fargo watched as Jody and Charles spoke, no smiles in their talking, their faces set and tight, and finally Charles turned and disappeared from view. Fargo watched Jody take two glasses from the table, vanish for a moment, then return. She started to shrug out of her robe, leaned over to blow out the kerosene lamp, but not before he glimpsed lovely bare shoulders and the upturned curve of her breasts. The house went dark and Fargo rose to his feet.

He made his way silently through the trees to the pinto, his face grim as he swung into the saddle and slowly started back the way he'd come. The words no longer froze on his lips and he heard his muttered rasp. "Damn little bitch. Sold me a bill of goods, she did," he said. And what else? he asked silently. Everything had taken on new shapes and new forms.

Jody Tanner had woven a story for him while the real truth lay masked. One thing had become fact. Jody, the lieutenant, and probably Charles were waiting for something damn important. Whatever it was, it was planned to come under cover of a wagon train. But they weren't the only ones waiting. Someone else waited and watched for that wagon train. Why? What did they wait for? What was so damn important? Where did the army fit? And Jody and the old man? They made a strange trio.

One other fact had remained. He'd been right all along about reasons for massacres and masquerades. Not just ambition or greed. The stakes were far higher. His mind held on Jody as the pinto climbed the slope toward the balsams. In a few, swift moments she had turned from a concerned seeker for truth, full of grief for a massacred brother, to a clever, lying little package. But she was apparently convinced that Amber was part of the wagon-train attacks. That was the one thing she hadn't lied to him about. And the real reasons stayed hidden, he swore softly. It was all suddenly made of undercurrents and the answer was somewhere on a wagon train. He'd find that answer, Fargo frowned. He'd find his way through the clever lies, the masks and under-currents. The innocent who'd been murdered deserved an answer and suddenly Amber wasn't near the question mark Jody had become.

He was still deep in thought, trying to find a handle, a new starting place, when he reached the camp and swung from the pinto. He caught the faint sound as his feet touched the ground and he cursed, spun, one hand reaching for the big Colt. But the blow came from the other side, almost directly behind him, the pistol butt smashing down hard. He fell, cursing the price of being too wrapped in thought. The world swam away in a series of circles and flashes, blue and red inner lights, and pain both sharp and dim. He felt the ground against his face, damp, loose leaves. He tried to move but nothing obeyed.

"No, not here," he heard a voice say. "Somebody might find him here." Fargo felt himself being dragged, loose dirt rolling over his face until he was lifted, flung bellydown over a saddle. Again he tried to move but failed to make even a finger respond. He attempted to open his eyes and failed at that, too, dimly felt the motion of the horse carrying him. The colors in his head had disappeared and he was wrapped in grayness now. A shroud? Was he suspended between life and death, on his way from one world to another? The thoughts floated lazily across his mind, as if generated on their own with no help from him. He didn't feel the horse's motion any longer and the grayness wrapped around him.

He didn't feel the horse finally halt, nor did he feel himself pulled from the saddle. Sensation suddenly came again as he struck the ground and he lay there motionless. Pain, first, and he fought away the throbbing in his head, pressed his hand against the ground. His fingers dug into the earth. He kept his eyes closed, the cry of joy inside himself. The pistol butt had struck a nerve someplace, knocking him out and robbing him of all sensation. Hitting the ground again had jarred the nerve fibers back into sensitivity.

He heard the voices again, clear now, nearby, kept his eyes closed. His fingers pressed the earth again, felt wetness, moisture, and his hearing began to return, sounds of water, soft lappings against a riverbank. He felt himself being lifted. Two men, one holding his legs, the other his arms. He felt himself being swung, once, twice, then sent sailing into the air. He kept his eyes closed as his body hit the water, cold shock, wetness coursing over his face at once. He let himself go limp, wanted the water to carry him swiftly downriver, drew in a deep gulp of air. But he wasn't going downriver. He felt the water pressure increase, the silence enclose him. He was plunging toward the river bottom and he snapped his eyes open, saw his ankles together moving downward, the rope around them attached to a boulder.

He bent his body forward, reached down to his leg, felt the leather strap around his calf, and drew the double-edged blade from its thin leg holster. His lungs were starting to burn as he used the sharp edge of the blade on the ankle ropes securing the boulder. He felt the river bottom, the boulder sinking into it first, went down on his knees. His lungs were fire now, his chest constricted. He worked the blade feverishly, felt it shredding. They'd used old rope and he was grateful for that. He expected his chest to burst apart when the rope suddenly gave way to let him propel his body upward.

The river was not deep and only that had saved his life, he knew, as he burst onto the surface to gulp in great drafts of air.

He treaded water as he let his lungs begin to breathe again, carefully drew in more air. The two men hadn't waited, the riverbank empty and silent in the half-moon's light. Fargo let the river push him to the bank, pulled himself up onto the soft earth, and lay there, letting his lungs drink in more air. He waited till he could breathe without hurting before pushing himself to his feet. He took the slender knife, the kind called an Arkansas toothpick in some places, and pushed it into his belt as he scanned the riverbank. Two horses with a third following. They wouldn't be all that far ahead, he saw, tracks showed them riding leisurely.

He turned and began to follow the tracks, using the long, loping gait that devoured ground. He was surprised when he caught up to them quickly and saw one reason. They had his pinto behind, the horse balking with each step. He moved into the trees, silent as a wraith. The two men rode side by side, he saw, let himself move abreast of them on padded footsteps. They'd taken his Colt, no doubt had it with them. It was too fine a piece to throw away. Fargo's eyes moved over the two horsemen as he trotted through the trees in step with them. He didn't recognize them, both wearing long sideburns on hard-set jaws. He wanted answers, but they'd shoot instantly, he knew. His mouth grew into a thin line. He'd have to settle for one.

He increased his pace ever so slightly, drew ahead of the two horsemen. His hand closed over the hilt of the thin, double-edged blade, drew it from his belt. He suddenly halted, half-crouched, took a split second to aim. His arm rose, shot forward, and the thin, double-edged blade shot between the trees with such speed it left a faint whistle of air behind it. The nearest rider turned his head just as the knife arrived. The blade hurtled through his larynx, stopping only when the hilt struck his neck. He half-rose in the saddle, suddenly looking not unlike a toy figure with a wind-up lever sticking from it. A guttural rasp came from him before he pitched forward as breath, blood, and life gushed from his throat. As he toppled forward from the saddle, Fargo saw the other man dive sideways from his horse, not waiting to draw a gun. He hit the ground and Fargo listened to him roll into the brush and trees.

The horses came to a halt a dozen feet on, and Fargo dropped to one knee, ears tuned, waiting. The rustle of brush broke the moment's silence as the man moved; Fargo shifted to his right, a noiseless shadow, came against the thin trunk of a young silver birch.

"You can stay alive," Fargo called softly. "A few answers will buy that for you."

His reply was two bullets that slammed into the bark of the tree. He heard the man drop low, push back into deeper brush. Fargo bent down and moved from the thin trunk on silent steps, circling to his left. The half-moon filtered a dim light through the trees and he let his gaze slowly move along the ground, halted as he found the dark bulk crouched by a tree. He started forward and disturbed a field mouse. The little creature scurried off with its usual noisiness and Fargo flung himself flat as the man blasted three shots with admirable speed.

Fargo lay flat, his cheek against the forest floor, the sound of the shots still ringing in his ears. He picked up another sound, a cylinder being flipped open. The man was reloading. Fargo leaped up, raced forward, started to fling himself at the dark bulk when he saw the gun come up. He flung himself sideways, twisting his body in midair as he cursed the man's quickness. Three shots whistled through the air and he felt one crease his shirtsleeve as he hit the ground, rolled, avoided another shot that kicked dirt into his face, continued to roll until he halted at a tree trunk. He heard the sound of the cylinder again. Damn, Fargo swore, the man was smart. He kept reloading, but he slipped in only three or four cartridges, cutting precious seconds off the time to reload a full six-shot chamber.

Fargo jumped up, darted through the trees, leaping from tree to tree, and the man fired at once, shots slamming into the bark.

"Come on, boy, I'm reloading again," he heard the man call.

Fargo muttered an oath and took the time to race in a half-circle. Again the man fired as Fargo leaped from tree to tree. Four shots and the man reloaded. Fargo dashed, heard the man's oath as he realized Fargo was heading for the pinto. The man fired again and Fargo ducked low, the shots wild this time. He counted six as the man emptied the chamber at him, glanced back to see the man reloading as he ran. But Fargo had gotten to the pinto, dived, and reached out at the same time to yank the big Sharps from its saddle holster. He hit the ground with the rifle in hand as the man fired another volley of shots, and this time Fargo felt the pain as one bullet grazed his shoulder, scraping flesh just over the end of the shoulder blade. The man had reloaded instantly, another three bullets as he came in.

Fargo brought the rifle up and fired as the man started

to raise his revolver. The blast caught the onrushing figure full in the chest, and the man halted, seemed to hang in midair as he turned red, his chest disappearing in a scarlet deluge. With strange slowness, the figure sank down to the ground to become a pile of sodden clothing.

Fargo rose, cursed, softly. He'd have no answers from either of the two. He slid the big Sharps back in its saddle holster and walked to the pile of clothes staining the ground, bent down, and fished into the man's pants pockets. He found only some coins and he turned to step the dozen paces back to where the other figure lay lifelessly on the ground. The man had his Colt in his belt and Fargo took his gun back, retrieved his throwing blade before going through the man's pockets. Nothing, he grunted. As with the killer who'd slain Sam Bowdy, these two carried nothing to identify them. Someone was being very clever, taking no risks.

Fargo swung onto the pinto, turned the horse around. The two had bushwhacked him, thrown him into the river to finish him. He'd leave them for the bristletails, earthworms, and burying beetles.

He emerged from the trees onto a hillside, found his bearings, and began to ride back to his camp in the balsams, not a long ride. When he reached his camp, he dismounted, stretched out on his bedroll, his jaw set grimly as he let himself digest the night. The two men had been waiting with orders to kill him. They'd known exactly where he had camped. They could have been tailing him and noted the spot, he considered. But they could have been told, given place and time, a blueprint for killing. He heard Amber's words in his mind. "You just stay right here and I might ride this way, come dawn." The words hung before him. "You just stay right here . . ." the phrase repeating itself.

Had she planned it all? Everything calculated to ensure that he'd stay in place? Even the lovemaking designed to put him into a relaxed slumber? It fitted too damn well, Fargo bit out. Maybe he'd thoroughly underestimated Amber Holloway. She'd already shown she'd use sex to get her way. Had all her talk about changing been just that, only hollow talk? Were her moments of seemingly genuine surprise and quick, open answers all aimed at disarming him? She'd done a pretty good job of it, he admitted sourly as Amber's face formed in his mind, the amber eyes and soft round-cheeked lines, the quick moments of real warmth and real anger. He still didn't see guile in her. Damn, he swore angrily. He didn't usually read someone that wrong, but events were painting a very different picture of Amber Holloway. Maybe she was the best damn actress he'd ever met, he grimaced. Maybe the only time she'd really been honest was when he was screwing her.

He made a harsh sound. All maybes and guesses, and his thoughts went back to Jody. The night had certainly been one of surprises all around. But Jody, for all her deceptions and quick lies, wanted him around and alive to bring her the proof that she was right about Amber. Which of them had spun the most treacherous lies for him, he had to wonder. He was sure of only one thing: he'd be finding out.

He closed his eyes and felt the exhaustion sweep over him at once. He slept quickly, the Colt in his hand.

6

He lay awake as the dawn sun prowled along the distant hills, cautiously heralding the new day. He lay still, let the time tick on. He gave her an hour past the dawn and rose, his jaw set hard. He let his eyes sweep the slope below, but there was no sign of her. Had she simply changed her mind? Or had something stopped her from coming? He couldn't discard either possibility, but there was one more that fitted the night too well. Had she been certain he wouldn't be there? He felt the grimness inside him grow deeper.

He washed at a near stream and dressed quickly, munched on a half-dozen wild plums as he rode the pinto down the back slope and up to the vantage point. He dismounted, leaned against a red oak, and let his eyes scan the flatland below and sweep across to the distant horizons. The sun was rising into a noon sky when the frown dug into his forehead and his lips pulled back in a soundless oath. The column of dust rose over the distant trees, almost at the horizon line.

He leaped onto the pinto and sent the horse charging downhill onto the flat avenue of grassland, raced the pinto at a full gallop across the flat terrain. The sound of the horse's hooves drowned out the curses he flung into the wind, and his eyes stayed on the column of dust as the powerful horse cut time and distance.

He was nearing the horizon line when the dust column suddenly changed, grew dark, smoke rising up to mingle with it. "Goddamn," Fargo swore, the oath directed at himself as well. He hadn't expected the strike would come that far from the others, and he cursed again as he raced the pinto up an incline, crested the top to see the three wagons spread out in front of him, one burning. A pack of loinclothed riders were circling, swooping in to fire their arrows; eight or nine, he counted quickly as he drew the Sharps and sent the pinto racing forward. The attackers darted in at the two wagons from both sides and Fargo saw their horses, big browns, and bays, not an Indian pony among them.

"Bastards," he yelled as he fired the Sharps at one swooping horseman. The shot missed, but he saw the rider turn his almost-naked, reddened body to look back. As one, the riders broke off the attack, racing off in twos, heading for a stand of nearby trees, separating as they neared the tree cover.

Fargo slowed, reined to a halt by the two wagons. The attackers would scatter beyond catching in the tree cover with the start they had. He swung to the ground as three men climbed from the wagons, two women helping two more wounded men to the ground. He saw others emerge from the last wagon, and his eyes swept the lifeless forms that lay draped over the wagon sides.

"Rotten bastards," one man said. "They just came at us out of nowhere."

A thin, gray-bearded man put his rifle down and stared through eyes of shock. "They hit Jake Drizzard's wagon first, killed the whole family, then tore the wagon apart before putting the torch to it," he said.

The other man stared at Fargo. "They sure took off when you came. Never seen Indians run like that from one rider."

Fargo gave a wry grunt. "You're not likely to see it again," he said.

"No matter, we sure owe you, mister," the man said.

"Let me look through your wagons," Fargo said, and the man frowned. "I want to see what you're carrying."

"Just personal possessions," the man said.

"I want to see for myself," Fargo insisted. "You said you owe me. That's all I want from you."

"Go and look, mister," the man said. "We've nothing to hide."

As they watched, Fargo went through both wagons, examined the household possessions, had an old trunk opened, and satisfied himself that it contained only clothes. He went through both wagons carefully and faced the curious stares of the pioneers when he finished.

"What were you looking for, mister?" the gray-bearded man asked.

"I don't know," Fargo answered grimly. "But I know it's not pots and pans and old clothes." He let his tone soften. "I thought you might be carrying something you didn't even know about."

"Something those redskins were after?" the man asked.

Fargo nodded, swung onto the pinto, and turned off

further explaining. "That bunch won't be back," he said. "Stay on guard, though."

"Thanks, again, mister." The man nodded as he watched the big man on the Ovaro ride briskly away.

Fargo didn't push the horse. He'd done enough hard racing for one day, but he maintained a steady pace. He wanted to reach Amber Holloway's spread as quickly as he could, a dozen probing questions digging at him. But it would be a time more for looking than for asking, judging more than concluding.

The early afternoon was waning when he rode into the ranch, his glance sweeping the acres of corrals. He reined up before the ranch house and watched Amber come out, her shirt tucked up to form a bare midriff over riding britches, the long-waisted figure moving with easy grace. He watched her as she came up to him, a hint of a smile toying with her lips. He swung down from the pinto, let his glance sweep the corrals again. He saw only two hands running feed into troughs.

Amber halted, hands on her hips, and there was no mistaking the smile touching her lips, a teasing, coy smile. "You angry because I didn't show this morning?" she asked.

"Now, why'd you think a thing like that?" Fargo returned.

"Your face is hard as a rock," she tossed back smugly.

He grunted, his face unchanging. "Why didn't you come?" he asked.

"Decided not to," she flounced. "You've had your way too easy. You've too big a head now."

He turned her answers in his mind as he watched the pleasure dance in the amber eyes. Had that been it? A

92

piece of sudden coquettishness, a need to show her independence? Damn, she was hard to read, he muttered inwardly. "Where's Ken Dixon?" he asked casually. "It's awful quiet around here."

"Ken went off early this morning, took most of the men with him," Amber said. "He's gone to see if he can get some horses for the wagons if the others don't get better soon. I don't expect he'll be back till late this afternoon," Amber said.

Fargo's face stayed stone, but the thought flared instantly inside him. Very convenient, it was, a hunt for spare horses, a perfect excuse for him to disappear with most of his hands. Fargo scanned Amber's face and he swore to himself again. It was impossible to read anything in that bland, unconcerned face that seemed entirely open. He pulled himself onto the pinto. "I'll be in touch," he said.

"When?" She smiled.

"Whenever," he growled.

He saw her eyes staying on him and the tiny giggle escaped her lips. "You all are angry," she drawled, and looked pleased again. "Maybe I'll come see you tonight, after the hands are bunked in," she said with a touch of clandestine glee in her voice.

"Won't be there," Fargo said.

Her eyebrows lifted. "Where might you be?" she asked.

"Visiting," he said, deciding to spear some on his own.

He saw the amber eyes darken at once. "Visiting?" she slid out, an edge creeping into her voice. "Visiting Jody Tanner, perhaps?"

He let a tight smile touch his face. "Now, that's not any of your concern, is it, Amber, honey?" he asked.

"Dammit, Fargo, you promised me you'd stay away from her," Amber snapped.

"I promised you I wouldn't work for her," he corrected.

"So why are you going to visit her?" she pressed angrily.

"Work's one thing. Play's another." He grinned.

"You all go to hell, Fargo, you hear me?" Amber flung after him as he rode off. "You can forget about my coming to see you ever again," she called after him.

He waved a hand without looking back. He hadn't lied to her. He intended a visit to Jody, but right then and there he guided the pinto up a slope and along the top land till he spied the stand of bur oaks. He dropped down to the road, cantered up to the house that continued to look bullfroglike across the end of the roadway. The day was starting to edge dusk, he took note as he reined to a halt and swung to the ground.

Jody emerged looking agitated, the new-wheat hair swinging from side to side as she half-ran to him, the upturned curve of her breasts bouncing little points into her light-tan shirt. "There was another attack, but you know that, of course," she said.

He let himself look surprised. "How do I know that?" he returned calmly.

"The survivors met up with Lieutenant Richardson and his men. They told him of a lone rider on an Ovaro coming to their help," she said.

"And the lieutenant reported right to you, did he?" Fargo smiled.

He watched her pull her face into cool containment. "He passed this way and stopped to tell me," she said. "Cheyenne, this time?" she asked.

He shook his head. "Nope," he said.

"Why are you so sure this time?" she prodded.

"Their horses, and the fact that they hightailed it the minute they saw me," Fargo said. "No Cheyenne raiding party would do that. This bunch didn't dare risk my bringing one down." He paused, leaned on the hitching post. "But they didn't get anything. I looked over the wagons," he said mildly.

Jody's mouth dropped open and she blinked before she caught hold of herself. "You looked over the wagons?" she echoed.

"Right." He nodded calmly.

"Exactly what does that mean?" she asked, unable to keep sharpness from her voice. "What did you think you'd find?"

Fargo held casual reasonableness in his face, choosing the words to fit his purposes. "Valuables," he said.

He saw Jody's eyes narrow at him. "Valuables," she repeated. "Just what do you mean by valuables?"

"Any kind, I'd guess." Fargo half-smiled. "Hell, I can't buy your ideas about Amber Holloway having folks killed to keep land clear and free for herself. I figure the bunch pulling these raids are trying to find a wagonload of valuables. Some of these folks coming from back east bring a lot of fine things with them."

He caught the mixture of relief and apprehension that flooded her face. "No, you're quite wrong," she snapped. "It's Amber Holloway's operation. It's exactly as I told you. You'll find out I'm right. Fact is, I was wondering why I hadn't heard from you," Jody said.

"Hadn't found anything to tell," he said, then paused, let his lips purse in thought.

"What is it?" Jody pushed at once.

"Just thinking that Amber's foreman and most of her hands were off someplace today," Fargo said.

"God, that's as good as proof right there," Jody said excitedly. "That wagon train is attacked and her men are off someplace."

Fargo laughed. "Jody, honey, you've got some funny ideas of proof," he said.

"You can't just dismiss it," she countered angrily.

He smiled and pulled himself onto the pinto. "I don't dismiss anything," he said. "Not even old Charles." He watched the alarm come into her frown.

"What do you mean by that, Fargo?" she asked.

He kept his smile as he put the pinto into a slow walk. "Damned if I know," he chuckled.

"Fargo, you come back here," he heard her call. "I want to know what you mean by that."

He didn't look back.

"Fargo, dammit, don't you play games with me," she called after him.

He continued down the road and the smile left his face. He'd tossed her just enough and caught the alarm in her at once. He'd been cryptic with a purpose. She'd fret and sweat, wonder and worry, over his remarks. They all would, because she'd tell the others, he was certain. It was exactly what he wanted, to bring her out, make her make a mistake. It was time to make things happen. When the time came for all hell to break loose, and he was certain that time was coming, he wanted to have his own plans ready.

He turned the pinto, broke into a trot, and headed across the foothills, riding west. He rode till the day neared an end, paused to watch two small Cheyenne hunting parties, gave them room, and continued on, using his uncanny memory for trails and marks to pick up the route he'd used when he followed the two Cheyenne bands a few days back. The dusk had begun to turn the light deep purple when he sniffed the air, his nostrils picking up the scent of campfires, venison being roasted.

He proceeded more slowly, stayed in thick tree cover until he glimpsed the encampment, three fires going, squaws beating elk hides, at least two dozen of the broad-base, distinctive Cheyenne tepees. No council camp but plenty large enough for his purposes, Fargo noted and guessed at perhaps seventy-five to a hundred braves. He carefully backed away in the darkness, mounted the pinto, and made his way back through the hills. He rode unhurriedly, let his mind form his plans, contingency plans in case he needed them.

The half-moon was high in the sky when he reached his second destination of the night, offering enough light for his needs. He reined up outside Amber's sprawling corrals, slipped to the ground, and scanned the ranch. The bunkhouse was dark, a small glow of light seeping out from somewhere inside the ranch house. He left the pinto outside one of the side corrals and circled on foot toward the stable, keeping to the corral fences until he reached the high-roofed stable structure. He ducked under fences, reached the stable door, slid the latch aside, and slowly pushed the door open. He halted, winced at a sudden creak from the door, stayed motionless, listening, heard only the sound of the horses inside. He slipped into the building, the rows of stalls before him, two rows in the center, additional stalls against the walls. A dim light managed to slip through a window as he started his way up and down the two center rows of stalls. He passed the cow ponies, a mule, a fine-bred gray mare good for pulling a cabriolet or a ladies' stanhope. He found the six horses he sought in the row of stalls against the far wall, strong-legged coach horses with maybe a little Cleveland bay in them.

He let whispered words soothe the animals as they grew instantly restless at his presence. He talked to them for a few moments, waited till they grew calm, then slid into the first stall. He bent down to look at the horse's forelegs, ran his hands up and down the tendons, paying special heed to the cannon bone, did the same with the hindlegs. He felt the hardness come into his jaw as he rubbed the animal's legs again and put his hands to his nose. No smell of liniment, not a trace, certainly no scent of the oil of wintergreen Dixon had said he'd been using. Oil of wintergreen stayed for weeks, he grunted.

Fargo went into the other stalls, did the same with each horse, finally straightened up at the last stall. No lameness in the horses—no lameness and no liniment that might have treated lame legs. There wasn't a damn thing wrong with the horses. It had all been an excuse to keep the wagons from moving out, and Fargo felt the frown dig at him. He couldn't figure it, but it had to fit someplace. He'd not try to put it in place here, he grunted as he started from the stall. The creak of the door cut through the soft breathing of the horses and he froze in place.

"Who's in here?" he heard the man's voice call, pressed himself against the wooden edge of the stall, and saw the figure move into the doorway. "I shut this door, Jeb," the man called, and Fargo swore silently. Two of them. "Someone's in here, Jeb," the man said, and stepped forward. Fargo saw the other figure come into the stable, shorter but broader. "You take that side, Jeb," the first man called, and started down the aisle between the stalls.

Fargo crouched, moved from the stall, grateful for the straw on the floor that deadened sounds. He backed along the outside of the stall, saw the first man moving slowly along the stalls, pausing to peer into each. He wore no gun belt, Fargo noted, but he carried a length of lead pipe in his hand. He glanced at the other aisle, saw the shorter figure moving down, also pausing at each stall, and Fargo saw the glint of gunmetal from his hand. Damn, he swore. He didn't want noise, shots that would bring the whole bunkhouse on the run.

The one with the lead pipe was moving more slowly, checking each stall more carefully. Fargo continued to back along the side of the last stall, dropped low as he spotted the pitchfork in a corner.

He stayed low, crossed to it in three long, crouching strides, and sank back into the corner. The short, broad figure with the gun in hand was almost on him. Fargo braced his legs, gathered the power in his heavily muscled calves. He held the pitchfork out in front of him as he stayed in the crouch. He could see the top of the man's head as he halted at the last stall in the row, peered into it and stepped on, stopped in surprise as he came face to face with the shadowed shape crouched in the corner. He started to bring his gun down, open his mouth to call out, when the shape hurtled forward with the force of a spring uncoiled. The man's mouth stayed open but a deep, guttural gasp came from it as the pitchfork slammed into his belly, both prongs driving deep. He went upward into the air as Fargo lifted, and the guttural gasp became a sucked-in wheeze of searing pain and the gun fell from his hand.

"Jeb? What's the matter?" Fargo heard the first man call from the other aisle. He dropped the pitchfork and the figure fell to the floor with the tool sticking up into the air out of his belly. Fargo heard the other man's footsteps racing around the end of the aisle. He stepped back as the man skidded to a halt, shock in his face as he saw the figure on the floor. He glanced up as Fargo tackled him, sending him crashing against a stall.

Fargo heard the lead pipe drop, lifted a blow to the midsection, but the man managed to twist, take it in his ribs. He was strong, the kind of wiry power that could surprise, and Fargo felt the man fling him backward, bend and scoop up the lead pipe.

"Son of a bitch," the man hissed as he came in, swinging the pipe.

Fargo ducked and saw the pipe smash a hole into the wood side of the stall. He started to step in with a short right, but the man was young and fast, brought the pipe downward in a chopping blow, and Fargo had to twist away. He felt the pipe graze his arm and he ducked again as the younger man charged forward, swinging his weapon.

Fargo feinted with a left, but the man responded at once, brought the pipe down in a fast arc where he thought to smash into an arm. But he flailed air, was off balance for a second, long enough for Fargo to bring a sweeping roundhouse blow that smashed the man along the side of his face. The figure fell sideways, against a stall, tried to turn, but Fargo's blow looped in low and came up against the point of his jaw. The man, still on his feet, half-rolled along the outside of the stall, and

Fargo, aiming, drove a vicious right to the face, which sent the man toppling to the floor. The pipe rolled from the man's fingers as he shook his bloodied head, tried to get up, and fell backward again.

Fargo stepped over the figure, started for the door, and felt arms wrap around his leg. He stumbled, almost went down, but twisted free and saw the man stumbling to his feet. The Trailsman turned, swung a final, short, chopping blow that seemed to separate the man's jaw from the rest of his face. The figure fell forward and lay shuddering on the stable floor. But Fargo was already running to the door, halted to peer outside, then darted into the night and around the rear of the stable to where he'd left the pinto. He vaulted onto the horse, forced himself not to gallop, and held the steed to a careful walk till he was far enough from the ranch to send the mount racing.

He swore silently. It was pretty damn certain the man had recognized him. Not that it would matter much now. He was all but sure that Dixon and the other hands were the fake Cheyenne raiders. They had a place where they went to bronze their bodies, put on Indian scalps and loincloths, change into Cheyenne warriors, the disguises good enough to fool terrified families fighting for their lives. When they finished, they returned to where they'd shed their clothes, cleaned themselves off, and hid their props away for another time. The process would take the better part of a day, he guessed.

Jody had been right about that much, it seemed, he mused. The fake Cheyenne came from Amber Holloway's operation. But the pieces still didn't fit together and he wondered why Jody Tanner was so sure she was right when she'd given him such phony reasons. He pushed away thoughts as he reached the balsams, dismounted, and put his bedroll against a tree at his usual campsite. He made a very small fire and stepped back. They would try once more to get him. They almost had to. Ken Dixon would know only that the big black-haired man knew more than he wanted him to know, but that was enough for another quick try at silencing him.

Fargo went into his saddlebag and took out a small wooden spool of mending thread. He pulled the big Sharps rifle from its saddle holster and went into the brush with it, beyond the tiny circle of dim light cast by the little fire. He rested the Sharps on the ground, propped it up steady with two stones, aimed it across the center of the fire. He took the mending thread and tied it to the trigger, returned and got the pinto, and moved a half-dozen yards into the blackness of the brush and trees. He paused to place the end of the length of mending thread on a flat rock, weighted it down with another. He found a broad tree trunk and sat down against it, let thoughts roll through his mind, determined to see if he could fit the pieces into something that might make sense.

He'd start at the very beginning, he decided. Amber Holloway had contacted him, hired him to take her wagons through Cheyenne country with her fancy hides. She must have intended to make the trip, he reasoned. There'd been no damn reason for her to send for him otherwise. Yet when he arrived there was the excuse that the horses were lame, the wagons not ready to roll. Why?

Fargo let the question dangle. It seemed to make no sense at all, and yet, his eyes narrowed, maybe it did. It was clear now that Dixon knew something was coming this way under cover of a wagon train, the same something Jody and the army waited for. But the timetable had gone wrong. The wagon train they all wanted hadn't arrived when he came onto the scene. Amber's wagons couldn't go out. Excuses had to be quickly pulled together so Dixon and his men could stay on. They had to play for time to continue their raids as the Cheyenne and try to get what they so desperately wanted.

But he had come along to change the picture, Fargo reflected. Until he'd arrived, Jody and the others were convinced it really was the Cheyenne raiding wagon trains. When it became known that he knew better, he was marked for killing. Sam Bowdy flashed through his mind. The man had obviously known what was going on and had decided to tell. He'd been killed for the attempt, and once more Fargo wondered about a killer so dedicated he took his own life rather than talk.

The picture had taken on outlines but little else. Reasons, motives, the heart of it that would make it make sense, still lay masked. It was indeed a strange passel of characters that lied, deceived, and murdered: a girl with new-wheat hair, the army, and an old man on one side; an open-faced, amber-eyed girl and her hard-jawed ranch foreman on the other. Fargo's lips pulled back in wonder. What in hell did they seek with such consuming desperation? What were the stakes for massacres and masquerades?

His thoughts held on Amber. Was she part of it? The very clever, cold-blooded mastermind? Or was she a pawn of some kind, unaware of the forces at work around her? He found his thoughts instantly flicking to his last night with Amber Holloway, when she had told him to stay and wait her dawn return. Two killers had come that night for him and the sourness welled up inside him again. Amber had started out as a question mark. Now she was a deadly riddle, one he couldn't risk guessing wrong about.

He pushed aside further thoughts. He could fill in no more of the picture until he had that final piece that still lay hidden on a wagon train somewhere. Besides, he caught the faint sounds drifting up the slope, little trails of dirt sliding downward, dislodged by careful, climbing boots.

He rose and crept toward the embers of the little fire. He dropped almost flat to the ground when he reached the spot where he secured the length of mending thread. He took the rock from the thread, twisted the end of the thin line in his left forefinger, and his right hand drew the Colt from its holster. He waited, almost amused. These were clumsy, moving too quickly. He saw the first figure appear, a second following, both with drawn guns. The two men crouched, peered at the fire, let their eyes travel around the edges to where the bedroll lay against a tree. They waited, listened, finally rose to their feet. One walked cautiously forward as the other hung back. "He's not here," the man said.

"He's here," Fargo said quietly from the blackness of the brush.

The man whirled, brought his gun up to fire, and Fargo yanked the thread around his finger. The big Sharps exploded from one side and Fargo fired from the other. His shot with the Colt caught the nearest man in the shoulder, sent him falling in pain. The shot from the Sharps hit nothing, but the second man fell backward at the blast, cursing in surprise and fright.

Fargo heard him falling down the slope, and he rose,

listened, heard the one he'd wounded half-falling, half-sliding after his companion. Fools sent on a man's errand, he muttered as he rose, holstered the Colt. They'd not be back, and Ken Dixon would be left wondering how much he knew. The man was no fool. He'd not move openly, not yet. He still had to lay back and wait. To Ken Dixon, Fargo realized, he was a danger but not a goal, and Dixon would keep his priorities in order.

Fargo took up the Sharps, pulled the mending thread from the trigger, and put the rifle back in its long saddle holster. He took his bedroll, moved another dozen yards back into the thick of the balsams, and lay down. Before he slept, he wondered again what kind of stakes could bring such cold-blooded ruthlessness, such dedication, deceit, and desperation. He fell asleep, still wondering.

The morning sun took its time filtering into the deepness of the balsams and Fargo enjoyed the extra sleep. When he woke, he freshened up with his canteen and led the pinto out of the trees. The sun was hot already, the hillsides lush and green in its glow. He scanned the rises and valleys, his eyes narrowed, caught a movement of foliage, followed it, glimpsed a lone horse and rider. He swung onto the pinto and sent the horse upward onto higher ground, fell behind the distant rider below, and caught the flash of new-wheat hair. He almost smiled as he watched her halt, peer up and down the slopes, turn her horse and head back the way she'd come. She halted every few hundred yards to frown across the land and he saw her squint toward the stand of balsams. She turned again, tried moving deeper into the hills, paused again to scan the land below. Fargo stayed back, moved the pinto in a line with her, and reined to a halt, his eyes growing narrow. He wasn't the only one watching her. He caught the flash of sun on a silver wrist bracelet, saw the Indian moving his pony silently through the trees. Fargo peered past the bronzed figure to find the other two. They were higher in the hills than he was and there was no chance of making his way up to them without their seeing him. Not now, with their every fiber alert.

He turned the pinto, rode boldly forward, out of his own cover and down toward the girl on the horse below. He saw her hear him, turn, watch him come down toward her. The three Cheyenne had halted to watch also, he knew. Jody's eyes stayed on him as he halted before her. She looked bandbox fresh in a pink blouse and black riding skirt, her hair almost platinum in the sun.

"Looking for me?" He smiled.

"Yes," Jody said. "I knew you were camping up here somewhere."

"It's pretty damn dumb to come up here alone," Fargo said evenly.

"I found you," she said smugly.

"You found more than me," he said, and she frowned. "Don't look around, just go on talking to me," Fargo told her. "Three Cheyenne, the real kind, are watching. They've been following you for some while." He saw the paleness drain her face, but she kept her eyes on him. It took an effort, he knew. "They have the drop on us now. They could put a half-dozen arrows into us with ease. I've got to turn that around."

"How?" she said, and her voice was suddenly very small.

"Turn your horse and ride along with me, nice and easy," he said, and wheeled the Ovaro in a slow circle. He let the horse walk down an incline, guided it through a passageway of shale slabs. He felt Jody's tension as she rode beside him.

"They're watching, following, of course," she said.

"You can count on it," Fargo said, pushed ahead, and led the way into a glen with a mountain pond and a small waterfall feeding it.

"What a lovely spot. Too bad I can't appreciate it," Jody murmured.

"You will." Fargo smiled at her. "I'm going to ride on."

"And leave me here?" she said, alarm leaping into her face.

"That's right. When I'm gone, you're going to undress and take a nice, leisurely dip in that mountain pond. You're going to stretch, swim, show it all, honey," he said.

"You're crazy. You're setting me up to be attacked," she hissed.

"I'm setting them up," Fargo said. "They're going to see me leave and you undress. They're men, Cheyenne men, and they'll respond like any men would. They'll watch you, enjoy the sight, all their attention zeroed in on you. That's what I'll need. Sure, they'll move in sooner or later, but not for a while." She continued to stare at him. "It's our only chance."

"We could run."

"Maybe fifty yards before we're pincushions," Fargo said. He moved the pinto forward. "Do it up good, honey. The more you hold their attention, the better chance we've got." He didn't give her a chance to protest, think of alternative ideas. He sent the horse into a canter and hurried through the passageway of shale. He kept riding, aware the Cheyenne would watch him go. When he reached the bottom of the hill, he let himself climb a clear ridge where the Indians would see him continuing on. Once into the trees again, he swerved the pinto, sent the horse up a sharp incline, and began a half-circle, staying in tree cover, leaving distance between himself and the mountain pond. He pushed upward through a thick cluster of white ash that brought him up behind the slope that looked down on the pond. He rode nearer, dropped from the pinto, and went on alone. Pausing, he scanned the foliage and found the three Cheyenne, one nearer him and, above, the other two. All three were riveted on their pond below and Fargo crept closer until he could see Jody below.

He paused, watched as she rose, saucy upturned breasts pointing skyward, her body glistening with water. She sent a shower of spray into the air, turned in the water, her full hips lifting upward, and she kicked out with her legs, revealed a glimpse of the near-blond triangle as she turned over, let her full, round rear glisten in the sunlight. She dived under the water, came up blowing water, her breasts bouncing.

Fargo took his eyes from her with an effort and crept forward, his hand reaching down to take the thin-bladed throwing knife from its holster around his calf. The Cheyenne's attention was riveted on Jody, and Fargo crept a few feet closer, saw that the other two were closer than it had seemed. Fargo half-rose, drew his arm back, and the Cheyenne turned, the instinct of the wild, the sixth sense of the untamed that never completely failed. The Indian started to spring forward, but the double-edged blade was already hurtling through the air. It struck the brave at the dead center, cracking his breastbone. The Indian gurgled, tried to clutch at the hilt of the knife protruding from his chest, missed, and toppled forward.

Fargo had the Colt in hand, leaped forward as he saw the other two Cheyenne turn, both tall, flat-cheekboned faces with black eyes. They sprang into action instantly, moving almost as one, leaping down at him, both drawing tomahawks from leather thong belts, tossing the short, thick bows to the ground.

Fargo held the gun with his finger away from the trigger. He'd fire only as a last resort, unwilling to risk bringing others unless he had to do so. The Indians separated to come in on him from both sides. One wore a beaded headband and was the bolder of the two. He darted in first, swinging the tomahawk in a short, flat arc.

Fargo ducked back, brought the heavy Colt up, and slammed it into the Indian's wrist. The man uttered a grunt of pain as the hatchet fell from his grasp. He dived for it and Fargo kicked out, catching him on the side of the temple. As the Cheyenne sprawled, Fargo dropped into a crouch, felt the second Indian's tomahawk cleave the air just over his head. The man crashed into him in the follow-through of his blow, and Fargo felt himself go down. He kept hold of the Colt, saw the Cheyenne dive at him, and rolled as the Indian brought the tomahawk down viciously.

Fargo felt the earth shake as the weapon landed. He brought his own arm around in a backhand arc, smashed the Colt against the Cheyenne's cheekbone, followed through as the Indian half-rolled with a second short, chopping blow to the man's face. He threw himself sideways as he heard the other one coming, saw the Cheyenne bring his ax down with all his force. He saw the Indian's eyes widen in horror as the tomahawk split his companion's head almost exactly in half, the skull separating as though it were a watermelon sliced in two. The man shook his head and half-turned away as blood, bone, and organs showered up over him.

He fell from the remains of the other brave, rose with a roar of rage, the tomahawk held in both hands. He leaped over the body, the weapon held high, his fury giving him speed and strength.

Fargo held still, let the flying form almost reach him, and flung himself sideways. The Cheyenne landed hard on the ground but whirled at once, swinging his short-handled ax. Fargo sucked his midsection in to avoid one sweeping blow, half-turned, and kicked backward, his boot landing hard in the Indian's belly. The Cheyenne grunted, half-doubled over, and Fargo brought the Colt around in an upward sweep. The gun barrel caught the Indian on the side of the jaw and the Cheyenne fell to both knees, tried to get up at once, but the big black-haired man brought the Colt down with all the power of his shoulder muscles. The gun struck the Indian across the back of the neck and Fargo heard the snap of vertebrae, stepped back as the Cheyenne pitched face-down on the ground, twitched convulsively, and finally lay still.

Fargo straightened, drew a deep breath, stepped around the lifeless forms to gaze down at the pond. Jody was still swimming, turning, giving her very best. He walked back to the pinto, rode the horse down the slope and back up through the shale passage that led to the pond. He saw Jody stop as she saw him.

"Show's over," he said, and she sank down into the water, only her head lifted upward, her eyes closed, her face drawn tight in relief. Fargo scooped up her clothes, brought the pinto to the edge of the pond, and reached a hand to her. She took it and he pulled her from the water.

"Let's get out of here," he said. "Hit the saddle."

"My clothes," she began, and he cut her off.

"You're too wet to put them on. Let's move," he barked, watched her pull herself onto the horse. He led the way around the mountain pond, through a stand of maple, and watched as she rode beside him, magnificently beautiful in her naked loveliness, breasts bouncing merrily, as though that was how she was meant to ride. He halted in a sun-drenched glade and she slid to the ground, stayed pressed to the horse. "You ride well bareback," he said, grinning.

"May I have my clothes now? I'm dried off enough," she said.

He tossed the clothes to her, dismounted as she rushed into the garments. She was in skirt and blouse when he stepped around to the other side of the pinto and sank down on the warm grass. She came over, knelt down beside him, and her skin, still damp, clung to the blouse, outlining the little tip of each breast.

"You did well. I almost couldn't stop looking," he said.

The mist-blue eyes met his gaze and he saw the faint flush that covered her face, ran down her neck, and touched the swell of her breasts.

"It was strange. I suddenly began to feel terribly

stimulated," she said. "It was as though I were tempting death, flaunting in the face of danger."

"You were," he commented, saw the mist-blue eyes grow darker.

"Yes, but I was enjoying it. I felt aroused, somehow. I know now what a tightrope walker feels, the stimulation of toying with death," Jody said, and he saw the flush stay over her face.

"You're still aroused," he said.

"No," she said, too quickly.

"Yes," he answered, reached out, and pulled her to him.

She gazed at him, the mist-blue eyes clouded, her lips parted. He leaned to her, slipped his tongue through the parted lips, and a shudder ran through her as her arms lifted, went around his neck. He felt her mouth closing around his tongue, pulling, sucking. "Oh, Jesus," he heard her breathe. His hands dipped inside the blouse, pulled it open, and grasped the slightly damp breasts.

Jody came against him and he lay back on the grass as her hands groped at clothes, pulling herself free. He slipped his trousers off and she almost tore his shirt free. The little cherry-red nipples seemed to implore, lift upward, and he pressed his mouth over them, each in turn. He felt her hands reach down along his body, move quickly along the inside of his legs, and find the waiting, throbbing maleness.

"Ah . . . aaaah . . . ah, Jesus, Fargo," he heard her cry out, and she clasped her hand around him, twisted her hips, brought her pelvis around to lay over his hips. She drew her legs up against his sides and swiveled her hips as her hand pulled him to her, thrust him to the eager entrance. He heard her half-scream as the round, smooth tip of his organ found her moistness and she plunged herself down atop him, ramming him into her until he felt the very end of her against him.

"Iiiiii . . . oh, Christ, Fargo," she screamed, began to pump furiously on him as her head fell onto his chest, turned from side to side, and each time a sharp, gasping cry exploded from her lips. She rose and fell furiously, pumping on him with a frantic fervor. He clasped his hands over her buttocks, helped her ram down on him, and now only soft, half-gurgling sounds came from her. Suddenly he felt her hands stiffen against him, her furious pumping become an uncontrolled frenzy. She exploded atop him and her head lifted, her mouth came open, and she screamed, a rasping, throaty scream as ancient as the rocks and earth around her, as wild as the eagle and the cougar.

"Aaaah . . . ah, Jesus," she whispered in regret as she fell back to lay over him, ecstasy too fleeting. She stayed atop him, wanting him inside her, wanting the satisfying, filling feeling to stay. But finally she pushed her legs back, slid from him, and lay at an angle across his hard-muscled nakedness, her face against his chest, her breath still returning slowly to normal. He heard her words, half-whispered, a touch of petulant anger in them.

"I didn't come looking for you for this," she said.

"Didn't think you did," he answered. "Why did you come looking for me?"

She pushed herself to half-sit over him and he saw her begin to pick words with clever carefulness, a veil of caution slipping over the mist-blue eyes. "I was bothered by the things you said yesterday," she told him, and let herself look hurt. Maybe Amber was the

113

best damn actress he'd ever met, he grunted silently, but Jody wasn't all that far behind.

"You mean about Charles?" he asked innocently.

She nodded. "I think you don't believe what I told you about him?" she slid out.

"Go to the head of the class." Fargo smiled.

"Why do you think I'd lie to you about him?" Jody asked.

Fargo laughed inwardly. The question was more than it seemed. She was probing with it, trying to find out what, if anything, he might suspect.

"Beats me," he said, lifted himself onto his elbows. "Why would you?"

She glowered back, looked away from him. When she brought her gaze back to him, the veil had torn from the mist-blue eyes, and her lips tightened. "I can't say anything more," she said.

"You can't?" he questioned.

She nodded. "That's right. But you can be honest with me," she said.

"No shit?" Fargo said, let a short, harsh laugh follow. "You've got funny ideas about what honesty means, Jody."

He saw her turn thoughts in her mind. "All right, I'll admit I wasn't completely honest about Charles," she said.

"Hell, I know that. Tell me something I don't know," he tossed back.

Her mouth grew thin again. "I can't say anything else," she repeated.

He rose, reached for his trousers. "Guess that makes two of us, honey," he said cheerfully. He watched her start to dress as he pulled on clothes, her face troubled,

114

a furrow creasing her forehead. When she finished, she pulled herself onto her horse and he strapped on his gun belt, swung onto the pinto.

"I'll see you get out of these hills safely," he said, and she swung in beside him, rode in troubled silence until he halted in sight of the stand of bur oaks.

She turned to him, her face still dark and troubled. "Look, Fargo, I know I asked you to help me get proof on Amber Holloway, but maybe you ought to back off now," she said. "It was probably wrong of me to ask you in the first place."

He smiled pleasantly at her. She was concerned that he might be coming too close to the truth. She wasn't alone in that fear, he was certain. "Hell, no, sweetie. It's just getting interesting," he said.

"It's not your concern. It never was. I pushed you into it and I was wrong," she said, working hard at being sincere.

Fargo's jaw hardened and he saw Jody's eyes widen as she saw the anger flare in him. "You flatter yourself. All those innocent families massacred pushed me into it. They deserve an answer."

Her mouth tightened as she turned away, made no reply. She moved on, slowly, not glancing back. He let her go a dozen yards when he called after her.

"I like you better laying than lying," he said.

Her back straightened and she sent the horse into a canter as his laugh drifted after her.

7

Fargo had traveled the flat grass almost to the horizon line when he sent the pinto up into the high land that afforded a good view of the terrain below. Two of the grassy pathways came together and simplified the business of watching for wagon trains. He thought about the morning with Jody as he sat motionless in the saddle, his lake-blue eyes moving back and forth over the land below. She was more than a hard-nosed little package. The stakes, whatever they were, seemed to draw the same unswerving, unshakable stance from everyone involved. Again, he had the feeling of some deep commitment, a strange dedication to something that evoked everything from simple stubbornness to total ruthlessness.

But he had come to another conclusion, this one about wagon trains. Perhaps the cover was not an honest one. The thought had intrigued him since it first popped into his mind. A wagon train, but not one made up of honest settlers. Amber's foreman had hit every train that drew near. He'd little choice. He couldn't do less and risk the prize slipping through his fingers. But he'd come up empty-handed each time. And Richardson and Jody seemed to know only that what they waited for would come on a wagon train. The thought was well worth pursuing, Fargo had concluded, and he leaned forward in the saddle as he saw a trio of Conestogas appear.

He waited, watched the wagons pass and head north, women in plain dresses, hair tied back tight, the men in shirtsleeves, and lots of kids. He stayed in place as the Conestogas went their way. The afternoon sun had grown hot when a line of four wagons came out of the east, passed slowly, a dozen hogs being pulled along behind the last wagon. Families, he saw, plenty of kids again. He watched the wagons move westward.

The day was growing long when he spotted the two covered wagons moving westward, one behind the other, a man and a woman on each, both men driving. The women wore stiff bonnets that all but covered their faces. He watched as the two wagons turned, moved up to where a stream coursed along the bottom of a hill. They halted and both couples clambered down. The women knelt at the stream, drank from it, and splashed water up into their faces as he watched. The men did the same, then stretched out on the grass. They rested, hats off, for some fifteen minutes, the women sitting quietly beside them. Finally they rose and climbed back onto the wagons again. Fargo's eyes were narrowed as he watched the two wagons move on, a faint smile edging his lips. He moved the pinto, stayed in the high land as he followed the wagons.

Dusk slid quickly across the land and he watched the two wagons pull into a shaded place and come to a halt. The two men made a fire and Fargo saw the women start to use frying pans. He moved the pinto down toward the camp and he smiled now. A wagon train, two wagons and two couples, not all that unusual. Not every train was full of kids. But these two couples were a little unusual, he had noted. The women never took off their stiff-cowled bonnets, not relaxing beside the stream and not now beside the campfire.

He continued to move closer, the night now blanketing the land. He circled around to the back side of the trees and dismounted, knelt down, and watched the couples eat quickly. The bonnets stayed on the women and his little laugh stayed inside himself. The men doused the fire and the two couples retired to their respective wagons.

Fargo waited, let the dark and sleep take over the camping place. He half-dozed himself, let more than an hour go by before getting to his feet and moving toward the wagons. He held a length of lariat in one hand, his Colt in the other. There'd been too much killing. He didn't want more if he could do without it. Moving on silent steps, he reached the first wagon, went to the tail, and halted. The sounds of snoring came from inside. Carefully he pushed the canvas back from the tailgate opening, stepped into the wagon. The nearest figure lay on his back, a stubble of beard darkening a fairly young face. Fargo's eyes went to the other figure in the wagon, saw the calico dress and hard-lined bonnet piled beside it. He stepped closer, peered down at well-muscled shoulders, a flat chest, crew-cut hair, and a square face. Both men were snoring heavily.

Fargo nodded to himself, drew the Colt back, and brought it down sharply on the man's head. The snoring cut off and Fargo whirled to see the other man wake, start to push himself upward. Fargo brought the Colt down smartly and the man fell back on the mattress. Fargo turned back to the first man, pulled him over, and quickly tied his wrists behind him, then did the same with the other figure. He stepped from the wagon, froze. A figure stood beside the other wagon, a ladle in one hand as he drank from the water cask. The man stared at him in surprise for a frozen moment, dropped the ladle as he dived into the wagon.

"Shit," Fargo swore as he heard the man's voice inside the wagon, another male voice joining it. Fargo leaped to the ground as the two figures hurtled from the wagon, one from the tail, the other from the front, both carrying rifles. He dropped as the man nearest blasted a shot at him, then he rolled under the wagon and saw the second figure racing around the other end of the wagon. He half-turned on his back, waited, saw the man come into view. The Colt barked twice and the figure stumbled forward, tried to rise, and fell back.

Fargo spun, flung himself from beneath the wagon, using one heavy wheel to pull himself free just as the rifle shot blasted dirt from beneath the Conestoga. Fargo pushed himself backward along the ground as his eyes swept the area in front of the wagon. He caught the sound, the rattle of a key chain, brought the Colt up. He was ready when the figure leaped into view, blasting a volley of shots under the wagon. He fired and the figure staggered backward. He saw the man's arms drop down, the rifle fall to the ground, and a white undershirt take on a spreading red stain. The man swayed a moment longer and then sank to the ground.

"Damn," Fargo swore as he pushed himself to his feet. He pulled the canvas open at the tail of the first wagon. The two men inside were awake, stared at him. He yanked the first one out, then the other, flung them on the ground and watched them struggle to a sitting position.

"Where is it?" Fargo barked.

"You crazy or something, mister?" one man asked, the dark-stubbled face peering at him.

"Don't play games. Where is it?" Fargo demanded.

"We don't know what you're talking about, mister," the crew-cut one said.

"Of course not. That's why you travel dressed up in bonnets and dresses," Fargo said. He saw the two men exchange quick glances, their faces grow sullen as they lapsed into silence. He eased himself down onto the step at the tailgate of the wagon. "You've got until daybreak to tell me," he said. The rest of the sentence needed no finishing.

Again, the two men exchanged glances, but they made no sound. Fargo leaned back against the wagon, holstered the Colt. Waiting for death was not something many men could do well. The ticking minutes grew louder and louder until they became sledgehammer blows inside the mind, shattering resolve, smashing the sturdiest of principles. Only the very strong, the very dedicated, or the very unprincipled could stand fast.

Fargo relaxed, watched the two men through half-closed lids. Neither man glanced up at him, hardly glanced at each other. The night dragged itself to dawn finally, and Fargo saw the pink-gray tint the sky. He waited, let the dawn intrude more fully, and he saw the men look up, exchange glances, turn their eyes on him.

"I didn't want this. I don't want any more killing," he said. "Just tell me where it is."

The two men stared back at him, no sullenness in their faces, only a grim stubbornness. Fargo rose, turned to the wagon. He drew the double-edged knife out and ripped the canvas open, laid it back, and began to go through the interior of the wagon. He examined clothes, slit open mattresses, took the floorboards up, and found nothing. He stepped outside, saw the two men watching him with silent hatred in their eyes. He went around to the front of the wagon, ripped the front panel away, bent underneath to examine the axle gears. He crawled back, kicked the water cask open, and cursed in frustration.

He started on the second wagon, took it apart with the same thoroughness he'd done the first, and with the same results. A last piece waited, a toolbox, and he opened the lid, reached inside it, and pulled out hammers, awls, a wrench. He threw everything on the ground, reached in again, and drew out a pair of cutting shears, tossed it atop the other tools. He reached into the toolbox again and his fingers came into contact with something smooth, cool, pliable. He found an edge, pulled, and drew out a leather pouch.

His eyes went to the two men, and their angry, bitter stares told him he had found what he sought. He took the leather pouch to his horse, pushed it into the saddlebag, put one foot in the stirrup, and turned to the two men. "You're lucky. I know some who'd kill you," he said.

He pulled himself onto the pinto and sent the horse into a fast trot, headed upland in the new day's sun. A leather pouch, he grunted, and inside it something that made men forgo their humanity. He'd get to it, alone, undisturbed.

He rode on, took a leafy pass upward, found a glen

beside a gnarled oak, and reined to a halt. He dismounted, pulled the leather pouch from his saddlebag, and sat down on a flat rock made soft by a thick cover of white-tipped moss. A piece of rawhide thong formed the clasp on the pouch and he untied it, pulled the contents of the pouch out. He stared down at a sheet of paper, hand-lettered, neat lines marching down the length of it. He saw names, names and addresses, neat rows of them, and he stared in disbelief.

Maybe there'd been some mistake, he wondered. Maybe this wagon train was a decoy. He shook away the thought. Men didn't give their lives for a decoy, not even dedicated men. He spread the sheet out in front of him and slowly began to read the names that had been carefully letter on it.

James Thurbbel
Nashville—Tennessee

Sam Starwell
Roanoke—Virginia

Joseph Hapgood
Memphis—Tennessee

Howard Arledge
Birmingham—Alabama

John Cantwell
Atlanta—Georgia

Robert Stoddard
Decatur—Alabama

Orlon Fosster
Atlanta—Georgia

Hubert Ross
Charleston—West Virginia

Albert Alderman
Greensboro—North Carolina

Harold Jenks
Columbia—South Carolina

Edward Appleby
Vicksburg—Mississippi

Durham Bell
Hattiesburg—Mississippi

Carlton Knowles
Carthage—Missouri

Francis Lawlor
Wichita—Kansas

Desmond Carter
Muskogee—Oklahoma

There was a second sheet with only another half-dozen names, and he put the top sheet back over it and stared down at the piece of paper as it lay across the leather pouch. Incomprehension welled up inside him. He felt somehow cheated. Names, a list of names. Nothing else, except for the address for each. He stared at the sheet as though he could will it to tell him something. But it revealed nothing, an answer that was its own riddle. But these names were more than a riddle. They were soaked in blood. The stench of death and deceit was on them. The innocent had paid the price for their being here, and he'd find out what they were and what they meant, Fargo vowed in silent anger. He'd find the truth of them, and he had the feeling that the truth would cleanse away nothing. But then the stains of the innocent were always hard to cover over.

He was still staring at the sheet in his lap, almost transfixed in frustrated anger, his concentration too complete. He heard the rifle shot explode, but a fraction of a second before he felt the pain in his temple, the world suddenly circling as he pitched forward to the ground. He lay still, blinked, felt the moss against his face, and the world had stopped circling. The pain stayed and he felt a little trickle of blood coming down along the side of his face. The shot had only grazed him and he started to move, reach for his holster, but he heard the footsteps almost on him and he lay still. "Got him. Got the son of a bitch," he heard a voice say, recognized the rasp of the one with the dark stubble of a beard.

"I'll get his gun," he heard the crew-cut one say, and he cursed in silence. How they got loose mattered little now, but he'd made a mistake somewhere. He felt the hand start to draw the Colt from its holster, gathered his muscles, and waited a split second longer, saw the man's shadow lean over him. He flung himself sideways, slammed into the man's ankles, and the figure fell forward across him. Fargo reached out, got his hands around the man's throat, clung as the man twisted, tried to pull free. The man slipped, fell, slid down the moss-covered side of rock, and Fargo clung to him as a wet leaf clings to a stone, making it impossible for the other to get a clear shot.

He rolled into the brush with the man, fell with him across a log, stayed against him, his hands tight around

124

his throat. The man tried to strike, but Fargo was too close, the punches without real force. Fargo saw the man's face growing red, felt his leg lift, try to knee him. He grimaced, shook away the pain, and his fingers stayed locked on the man's throat. Fargo fell with his opponent again as the man went backward, hit the ground, and Fargo heard the man's throat hiss, felt his body go limp. He kept his grip on the man's throat until the dull veil of lifelessness slid over the man's eyes. It took him a moment to unlock his fingers, prying them loose with effort, and he half-crawled from under the man's body, listened, stayed quiet. There was no shot, and ears straining, he picked up the sound of the other man racing down the incline.

Fargo swore, leaped to his feet, and raced for the pinto. His gun was somewhere, but there was no time to search for it now. The other man had the leather pouch and its contents, he knew, and he wondered again what drove so many to such consuming selflessness. He reached the pinto, hit the saddle in a running bound, and sent the horse galloping down the incline. He spotted the man below, racing toward a pair of horses tethered side by side. The man flung a glance back at him, heard the pinto coming hard.

Fargo kept the horse charging, the dark-stubbled face only a few yards in front of him, and he saw the man drop the leather pouch, raise the rifle in his other hand. Fargo dived from the pinto's back as the man fired at almost-point-blank range, and the horse swerved away from the blast. Fargo hit the ground, came up on his feet, saw the man shoving cartridges into the rifle. He dived forward, came in low, hit the man at the knees before the figure could get off another shot. The man went down and Fargo went with him, drove his knee into the man's stomach, and heard the harsh gasp of pain. The man rolled onto his side and Fargo kicked the rifle that half-fell from his hands. He tried to bring a short, chopping blow down against the man's neck, but the figure surprised him by flipping over into another half-roll, toward the rifle.

Fargo moved quickly as the man's hands found the weapon. The trailsman brought his foot down hard onto the small of the man's back, felt a small bone snap, and heard the man's scream of pain. The man clung to the rifle, dragged it to his shoulder as Fargo kept his foot planted hard on the man's back. He watched the man, frowning. There was no way the man could turn to bring the rifle to bear on him, yet his fingers found the weapon's trigger. Fargo saw him point the gun waveringly, watched his finger tighten on the trigger, and suddenly, in horror, saw the gun was aimed at the leather pouch on the ground.

"Shit!" he swore as he pulled his foot from the man's back, kicked at the rifle, hit the end of the stock just as the gun went off. He saw the slug tear a hole in the ground inches from where the leather pouch lay. He reached down, yanked the gun from the man's hands, but he saw there was little need any longer. The man's eyes stared at him with the emptiness of the dead. Fargo pushed the body with his foot and it rolled lifelessly onto its side.

Fargo turned away, picked up the leather pouch, and felt the sense of awe and incomprehension well up inside him. The man had tried to destroy it, blow away its contents with his last act. It was the most important thing for him to do. The word swam across Fargo's mind again; "dedication," the single, consuming purpose. Dedication to what? Not to a set of names. His face set hard, his jaw muscles throbbing, he held the pouch tight against him as he walked to the pinto and put it into the saddlebag. He paused to glance down at the still figure. A length of lariat was still wrapped around one of the man's wrists. The end had been cut clean. They had taken the cutting shears he'd tossed from the toolbox, managed to cut each other's wrist ropes, unhitched the horses, and gone after him. He climbed onto the pinto and began the ride back, letting the horse walk. There was time. He had to wait for the night.

Richardson and his patrol would find the wagon. Perhaps Dixon also. It would be different than any of the others, and they'd wonder, worry perhaps. They'd both know the truth of it soon enough, Fargo muttered. He circled, giving the flat grassland a wide berth, stayed in the hills until the night came. He let the moon rise high enough to lay a pale light over the earth, and he turned the pinto toward Amber Holloway's sprawling ranch. He had decided Amber would be first. The bloody, fake Cheyenne raiders had come from her place. He'd find the answer to two questions at once.

He slowed as he finally came into sight of the wide-spread corrals, rode as close as he dared, and dismounted. He took the leather pouch, folded it lengthwise, and pushed it into his belt. The bunkhouse was dark, he saw as he dropped to one knee beside the first corral. There were no lights in the ranch house, either, and he slowly scanned the corrals, saw no guards posted. He began to make his way toward the main house, cut through two corrals to the rear of the house. He halted against the back door, carefully eased the doorknob into turning.

The door came open with a click so faint he hardly heard it himself and he released his grip on the doorknob, pushed the door open just far enough for him to slip into the dark house. He pulled the door closed enough to just rest against the latch and halted until his eyes grew used to the dark of the house. Moonlight through the windows filtered in enough light to let him see he was in a rear hallway, and he began to move forward on silent footsteps.

He paused to listen every few steps, finally heard the even sounds of her breathing. They came from a room just off the other end of the hallway and he reached it to find the door more than half-open. He stepped into the room, pulled the door closed after him, and saw the figure on the full-sized bed. She lay on her side, a sheet curled across her hips, and he was glad to see she wore a full-length, high-necked nightgown. The less distraction, the better, he grunted. He crossed to the bed in three long strides, glanced past the sleeping figure to the window, white curtains half-drawn. He leaned over Amber and pressed his hand over her mouth.

Her eyes snapped open instantly, became round and frightened as she stared up at him. "No noise," he murmured. "Promise?" She stared at him for a long moment, then nodded her head against the pillow.

He took his hand from her mouth and she sat up at once, her frown made of uncertainty as much as fright. He moved around the bed to the other side, drew the curtains over the window completely. "Put your lamp on," he said, and waited as she swung half out of bed and turned a bedside lamp on to a soft glow. Her eyes, wide with wonder, stayed on him as she sat at the edge of the bed.

"A bit late for a social call," she said with tartness.

His face was cold stone, his eyes equally so. "Stables one night, bedrooms another," he slid out, and saw the astonishment leap in her face.

"That was you last night?" she breathed. "I heard they surprised someone in the stables." He nodded and saw Amber's eyes turn accusing. "You killed one of the men. Why?" she asked.

"He didn't give me a choice," Fargo said evenly.

"What were you doing sneaking around in the stables?" Amber shot back.

"Getting some answers. Now I want the rest of them," he said, the hardness staying in his face.

Amber frowned. "What are you talking about?" she pushed at him.

He pulled the pouch from his waist, opened the leather thong, and pulled the sheet out, held it out to her. "This," he growled, and watched her peer down at it, her frown deepening.

"What is it?" she asked.

He made a harsh sound. "You tell me," he barked.

Amber continued to frown as she read down the list of names. He watched her as the eagle watches the rabbit, alert for any gesture, any motion, any tiny thing that would reveal more than it intended.

She looked away from the sheet, met his piercing stare. "Names, a list of names," she said. "I don't know what it is or means or anything about it."

"Try again," he flung at her through gritted teeth, grasped her face, and turned it to the list again.

"You're hurting me," she said, and he relaxed his grip. She stared at the sheet again, returned her eyes to him. "I don't know any of them, if that's what you're asking," she snapped.

"What do they mean, dammit?" he rasped.

"I don't know, I told you," she returned angrily.

He hadn't taken his eyes from her and she'd revealed nothing, no answers too carefully given, no cunning touching her eyes, no out-of-place fleeting expression, nothing. He swore inwardly, put the sheets into the pouch and the pouch behind his belt.

"Ken Dixon knows what they mean," Fargo slid at her.

"Now what are you saying?" Amber questioned.

"He's been pulling those fake Cheyenne raids," Fargo snapped.

He waited, saw Amber's mouth drop open, her face flooding with racing emotions, shock encompassing all others. If it wasn't the real thing, it was the best damn performance he'd ever seen, he swore silently.

"No," she breathed. "No, I won't believe it. It's impossible. You've got something wrong."

"Hell I do," Fargo growled. "He did the killing. Did you do the ordering?" He met her stare, saw the shock turn to anger in her eyes.

"You all get out of my house, damn you," she spit at him. "I don't believe any of this. Maybe Ken was right about you being a crazy man."

Fargo's hand shot out, seized her by the front of the nightgown. He yanked her upward, his big hand gathering the nightdress in a knot. "Don't you come on that way with me, honey. You're on awful thin ice. You give me answers, not orders," he said.

He saw fright push the anger from her face. "I don't know anything about any of this," she said, her voice growing almost quiet. "I don't believe you about Ken. It's impossible. Why would he do that?"

Fargo pressed the pouch at his waist. "For this, for whatever this means," he said.

"I don't know anything about that and I didn't give any orders about anything," she said, paused, eyed his stone face. "You don't believe me. You've never really believed me about anything, have you?"

He didn't answer, released his grip on the nightdress, and Amber stepped backward. He swore again silently. He was coming up with no answers, not about the meaning of the pouch and not about Amber. His eyes bored into her, saw a stubbornness coming into her round-cheeked face as she returned his gaze. His eyes stayed hard on her as his thoughts raced. There was more than one way to skin a cat. Maybe there was more than one way to answers.

"You check out those lame horses?" he asked suddenly, saw her taken by surprise at the question.

"No," she said. "Ken reported to me every morning on how they were doing. I'd no cause to check on them."

"They're not lame. Never were," Fargo told her. "Dixon needed time to stay here, to try and get his hands on this pouch. He used the lame horses as an excuse."

Amber sank onto the edge of the bed and seemed a lost little girl suddenly. "No . . . I can't believe this, not any of it," she murmured. "I don't know anything about it."

He stepped to her, bit out words. "You're lying to me. I'll be back for your lovely hide, honey. You can count on it," he said. She stared at him. "Turn out the

131

lamp,'' he said as he moved away from her. She leaned over and blew the lamp into darkness and Fargo crossed the room in three long strides, ran down the hallway and out the back door. He ran to the pinto and turned the horse down the road. But he halted before he'd gone a half-dozen yards, moved under a long-branched horse chestnut. He sat motionless in the blackness beneath the tree, his eyes riveted on the house.

He guessed not five minutes had slipped by when he saw Amber stride out of the house, a lantern in her hand. His eyes followed her as she moved through the night in a small circle of light. She walked quickly, purposefully, passed the corral to halt at the stable door. He watched her lift the latch and push the lantern inside ahead of her. He waited till she disappeared into the stable and turned the pinto, rode from beneath the tree in a fast canter.

Amber Holloway had just told him what he wanted to know. He quickened the pinto's pace as he reflected on the ways of life with a wry grimness. In one short walk to a stable door, Amber had said more than all her words of protest and denial could say. Actions still spoke louder than words. If she hadn't taken that walk to the stable door, if there'd been no need for her to check the horses, she'd have given the lie to everything she had said and done. She'd have given another answer, equally final. But she had gone to see the horses and he knew one thing now: somehow, she was part of it without being part of it, crazy as it sounded. How, was unimportant now. The final truth was all that mattered now. He rode across the hills to the stand of bur oaks, down the moonlit road, the anger hard inside him.

The house straddling the end of the road loomed up

darkly malignant—fitting, he thought. Jody Tanner had lied enough, woven enough tales, backed off for the last time. He slowed the pinto, his sixth sense suddenly flaring, and turned into the trees to approach closer. He halted as he saw the horse hitched outside the front door, the lone figure with the army carbine standing straight and trim before the entrance to the house. A grim smile touched Fargo's lips as he made his way to the side of the house, crept forward, crossed into clear space to a partly open side window on foot. He bent low, peered into the house, saw a small room, empty except for an old chair, and he slowly eased the window up enough to let himself crawl into the house. He halted inside, heard the hard half-snorts of an old man's sleep, and he moved down a short hallway past a closed door. He found the living room and the closed door leading from it. He drew the big Colt. He'd seen enough examples of the total commitment involved in this strange affair. He'd take no more chances. Besides, Jody could be a hard-nosed case, he recalled grimly.

He eased the door open, scanned the small room, the bed closer to the window than he'd remembered. Jody slept on her side, clothed in a pink nightgown, modest enough with a high, ruffled front that covered her breasts but left her shoulders bare. He stepped to the bed, pressed one hand over her mouth as he had with Amber. But Jody came awake very differently, grabbed for the hand over her face, swung out with her other hand in a small fist as she tried to twist away. He took the blow alongside his cheek and leaned down half across her, pinning her arms and body back.

"It's me, dammit," he hissed. He saw her blink, focus on him, and felt the stiffness drop away from her body. He saw her eyes go to the barrel of the big Colt he held in his hand alongside her temple. "No noise," he growled, and she agreed with her eyes. He took his hand from her mouth and stepped back.

She sat up as though on springs, anger flooding her face. "What the hell is this, Fargo?" she half-whispered.

"Get dressed," he said.

"Why?"

"We're going to have a talk," he said.

She frowned at him. "All this for a talk? You could come by anytime. You've done it before."

"This is a special talk," he told her.

"We can talk here."

"Not with your personal guard outside and old Charles in the next room," he said.

She tossed an annoyed glance at the Colt in his hand. "I'd hardly say you need that," she commented.

"Friendly persuasion," he snapped. "Dress."

"Turn around," she glared.

"No way, sweetie," he said. "I've seen it before. Your memory that bad?"

She threw him another glare, turned her back on him, and reached for her clothes. She slipped the nightgown off and pulled her shirt on in quick succession. He had but a quick glance at her firmly rounded little ass, but enough to stir memories. She had boots on in moments more, the black riding skirt wrapped around her.

"You first, down the hall to the side window," he said.

She obeyed and he stayed close behind her. She started to swing herself over the sill of the open window when they reached it and he caught her by the arm, his voice whispered steel. "Just so's we understand each other," he said. "You want to get that young trooper out in front killed, then you try calling him."

She met his eyes, he watched her accept what she saw in them, then she swung silently to the ground. He followed, took her arm, steered her to the trees as he kept his eyes on the front of the house. The soldier was still concentrating on the road. Fargo pulled the pinto around, gestured to Jody, and she mounted. He swung into the saddle behind her. He felt the softness of her rear against him and wished it were another time and another place. He sent the pinto through the trees until he was far enough from the house to take the road. When he veered into the hills, a faint pink line began to touch the tips of the high trees. She saw it just as he did.

"God, it's dawn," she said.

"Time flies when you're having fun," he bit out.

"What is all this, dammit? What's come over you?" Jody asked.

He didn't answer, his eyes searching the ground as the new day began to let the earth take on shape. He found a small open glade and halted, slid from the pinto. She followed and faced him, her mist-blue eyes dark with anger.

"How come the lieutenant decided to give you a personal sentry?" he asked mildly. "Couldn't be you told him some of the things I said yesterday? Is he getting nervous about me?"

She didn't answer. "You bring me all the way out here to ask me that?" she countered.

He turned to the saddlebag and pulled out the leather pouch, turned to her with his face hard stone again. He opened the pouch, drew the sheet of names out, and

135

held it in front of her. He watched Jody's eyes grow round as she stared at it, her words gasped out in an awed whisper. "Where did you get that?" she breathed.

"In a wagon train," he said, and she tore her eyes from the sheet of names to look at him, shock in her face. "A wagon train as fake as those Cheyenne," he added.

Jody's eyes went back to the sheet of names and she stared at it as if transfixed. He saw her hand reach out for it. "Give it to me," she murmured.

He drew the sheet of paper back. "Like hell," he said.

"It's not yours," she muttered, her eyes still staring transfixed at the list.

"It's not yours either, sweetie," he countered.

She blinked and it took another effort for her to pull her eyes from the list of names. "You don't understand, Fargo," she said. "Just give me the names and leave it at that."

His voice grew filled with ice. "No, *you* don't understand, Jody, honey. You're going to tell me what this goddamn piece of paper means."

"I told you yesterday, I can't say any more," she answered.

"No more of that shit, honey," Fargo barked. He drew the big Colt, held the list of names up in one hand, and put the end of the gun barrel against the sheet. "You talk or I'll blow this whole damn sheet of paper into little pieces."

"No!" The single word tore from her throat.

"I want the truth. I want to know about you, the army, and old Charles. I want all of it, you hear me,"

Fargo flung at her. "You've about three seconds before this gun goes off."

He saw her breasts rise, press hard against her shirt as she drew a deep sigh of resignation from inside herself. "All right, put the gun down," she said.

Fargo drew the Colt back from the sheet of paper, his eyes hard on Jody.

"You've heard there's trouble between the states?" she asked.

"I've heard some talk," he said.

"It's more than talk," she answered gravely. "The South has threatened to leave the Union, secede. That means war between the North and the South, the Union and the Confederacy, a civil war."

"The South hasn't quit the Union yet," Fargo said.

"President Lincoln is convinced they will, that it's only a matter of time or the right trigger to make it happen," Jody said. "That list of names was started a year ago. It's a list of those men in the South who will help the Union cause. They are Southerners who disagree with slavery, the secession, everything. Some are very important men. That's why we must have that list, Fargo."

"We?" he questioned.

"The Union, the President," she said. "When it was learned that the list was being prepared, Charles and I were sent out here to wait for it and to be a message drop."

"Why you and old Charles?" Fargo cut in.

"Old Charles is Charles Dodson, one of President Lincoln's closest advisers. I worked for Charles in his office. We knew Charles Dodson couldn't come out here and wait without arousing suspicions. There are southern spies all over Washington. So it was decided to send Charles and I out here in reverse roles, in disguise, you might say."

"With the army standing by to help," Fargo commented.

"That's right," Jody said, paused in thought, and went on. "We knew the South was aware of the list and wanted their hands on it. We didn't know they had information it was being sent here until you told me the Cheyenne raids were fake."

"So you figured it had to be Amber Holloway, her coming from Virginia," Fargo said.

"Of course. Her father's a very important man in Virginia," Jody said.

"You were only half-right. Amber Holloway isn't part of it. She came here to do her own thing. They used her as a cover. That's why her daddy gave her Ken Dixon, something she never understood. Dixon is their man here."

"No matter. Now you know," Jody said, her face grave.

Fargo nodded. It put all the little pieces together, an assassin that didn't act like a hired killer because he wasn't. The word swam into the Trailsman's mind again: "Dedication." People totally committed, dedicated to a cause. Nothing but the cause matters, on either side. He heard Jody's voice cut into his thoughts.

"Just give me the list now, Fargo," she said.

He brought his eyes to her, frowned, his thoughts about what causes did to people still revolving inside him. "No," he said. "It still stinks." He saw Jody's frown dig into her brow. "How many innocent men, women, and children have been killed because of your goddamn list?" he shot at her.

"You can't blame us for that," she protested at once. "They did the killing. They set up the fake Cheyenne raids."

"Yes, that's true enough, but you think you're lily-white in this, don't you?"

She said nothing, let her silence answer.

"The hell you are," he barked. "Your side thought up the wagon-train cover. You made every innocent wagon train a possible target. You knew they had wind of something. But you didn't care about that. Innocent men, women, and children make a good cover." He saw her lips press down on each other. "They did the killing, but you marked those people for it just as sure as if you'd put a cross on them. No, honey, you can't shake away your part."

"Fargo, give me the list and back away," Jody said. "You don't have to involve yourself."

Fargo felt his eyebrows lift. "Really, now?" he said. "You did every damn thing you could do to involve me and now you want me to uninvolve myself."

"Yes, I did," she admitted. "But it's over now. You don't have to get into it any deeper. Just give me the list," she said doggedly.

"No list, baby, not till I think some more on it," he bit out.

"Fargo, they want that list. They'll kill you for it, just the way Dixon will if he can. The lieutenant has his orders," Jody said.

"I'm sure he does. Did you have your orders, too? Did they order you to fuck me for it?" he flung at her. "Anything for the cause?"

139

Her eyes blazed at him. "Bastard. I don't do that on orders," she spit back.

"I'm not sure I buy that, Jody baby," he said, paused, grinned at her. "If I offered you the list for a final fuck right here and now, what would you say?"

"You rotten bastard," she threw at him, and he watched her breasts rise up against the shirt as she took in deep, angry gasps of air. "You lousy son of a bitch. I'm damned whatever I say the way you put it."

"Prove me wrong. Just do it, no promises on my part. Make me change my mind," he said, and saw her eyes narrow, thoughts leaping inside her.

"Bastard," she said softly as she began to unbutton the shirt.

Fargo put the pouch back in the saddlebag, looked at the new sun sliding over the little glen. He pulled off clothes and reached for her, saw the flush in her face, the same tingling in her she'd had after the time with the Cheyenne.

"Bastard," she murmured as she pressed herself against him, sank down onto the soft, dew-touched grass. His lips found one upturned breast, then the other, and he felt her legs opening at once, waiting, but he lay over her, letting his organ rest on the almost-blond nap. She sucked in breath, her hand reached for him as she lifted, tried to push herself against him. She was hurrying and not just with passion. He'd never really doubted that she'd wanted it the other times, but he had definite questions this time and all her deceits and evasions flooded over him. She had been part of the callous disregard for innocent lives and he felt the anger spiral inside him.

He drew back, held between her opened legs for a

moment, then rammed forward. "Aaagggh . . . Agh, Christ, Fargo," she gasped out as he thrust into the very end of her orifice. The moistness was only beginning to flow in her, but he rammed again, hard, anger pushing with each thrust.

"No, wait—aaaagh, oh, Jesus," she cried out. But he refused to wait, rammed and battered into her, and suddenly he felt the wetness flowing over him and she was pushing back with his every angry, ramming thrust. "Yes, yes . . . Jesus, oh, Jesus," she cried out. He wanted to punish her and he was giving her only pleasure now, and he realized the irony of victory. He slowed his angry thrustings, but she grabbed at him. "No, no . . . go on, go on," she implored. He returned to his harsh lovemaking until he heard her ultimate scream, anger and ecstasy in it, wanting and hating, pleasure and pain. It had been furious and made of strange heights, too quick, yet perhaps not quick enough, and she lay beside him breathing hard.

Slowly her eyes came open and she drew herself up on one elbow, lay half across his chest, her voice fuzzily soft. "Give me the list, Fargo. I don't want anything to happen to you," she murmured.

He smiled, sat up, and pushed back from her. "Time to get dressed, Jody," he said, reaching for his trousers. He had them on and she was still staring at him.

"What are you saying?" she asked ominously.

"No list, honey." He smiled almost ruefully. "Get dressed."

"Dammit, Fargo, you said for me to prove something to you. I did it, you promising nothing. Doesn't that mean enough?" she flung at him.

"It means you had nothing to lose by giving it one more try." He smiled cheerfully.

"You don't know that, dammit," she yelled at him. "That's unfair."

"Life's unfair. Innocent people getting killed is unfair." He shrugged.

"You never intended to give me the list," she shouted as she pulled on clothes.

He swung onto the pinto, waited for her to finish dressing, and pulled her into the saddle in front of him. "I'll take you back to your place now," he said.

"Lieutenant Richardson will be there," she snapped.

"I expect so." Fargo smiled. "When Charles found you missing, he figured something went wrong. He sent the trooper hightailing to fetch the lieutenant. They've had time to get back there now."

"You were marking time just now, that's all," Jody accused. "You no good bastard."

"I wouldn't put it that way, honey. I was enjoying myself. So were you." Fargo smiled.

Jody turned, frowned at him, searched his face. "Why are you taking me back where Richardson is waiting? You know I'm going to tell him you have the list," she said.

"I certainly do know that." Fargo smiled. "And by now Amber has had it out with Ken Dixon and he knows I've got the list. He'll be out with everybody he's got looking for me."

He saw the consternation in her eyes. "You trying to commit suicide?" she questioned.

"I might be, if I let Dixon and his bunch or the lieutenant and his troopers concentrate on me," Fargo said. "But they'll be chasing me with one eye on each other, ready to make sure that neither one nor the other gets to me first."

"Somebody will," Jody said. "You can't win."

"I figure to get some help," Fargo said. She turned again to frown at him. "Dixon's been playing Cheyenne. He's going to find out what the real thing is like. And the lieutenant will get to see what he's been looking for all month."

"You're going to lead them into a trap," Jody gasped. "You can't do that."

"Why the hell not, honey?" Fargo said, his voice suddenly razor-sharp.

"They're white men. They're your own kind," she said.

Fargo's laugh was harsh and bitter. "They may be white but they sure as hell ain't my kind," he said. He swung onto the road beyond the bur oaks and saw the house ahead of him. Charles stood beside the lieutenant, who had brought an augmented patrol, he saw, some twenty-five troopers. Fargo rode to within twenty yards of the house and brought the pinto to a halt. "This is where you get off, honey," he said, and Jody slid to the ground, cast another glance up at him, and he thought he saw real concern in her eyes.

"Give me the list, Fargo," she said quietly.

She turned away as the big black-haired man's eyes were focused on the lieutenant and his platoon lined up in front of the house. She didn't look back again, walked firmly toward the house. Fargo watched Richardson start to walk toward her, saw Charles Dodson's eyes on her. Suddenly Jody broke into a run. "He's got the list," Fargo heard her scream. "He's got it."

Fargo laughed as he spun the pinto around, sent the

horse into a full gallop. He looked back to see Richardson pulling himself onto his horse, waving his men forward. He could hear Jody's cry. "Wait. Don't go chasing after him," she called, but the lieutenant wasn't listening. He was leading his troopers in full pursuit and Fargo laughed again. He knew the lieutenant wouldn't listen to her, once he heard the magic words. Fargo moved forward in the saddle, concentrated on riding hard and fast. It would be a shell game with himself as the shell, and he had to make his moves exactly right or lose.

8

He headed up toward the balsams, rode along a ridge.
Richardson's troopers posed no danger yet. He had
enough of a start and their numbers made going uphill
slow. He ran the pinto along the ridgeline, saw the
troopers swing in behind him. He'd gone perhaps a
quarter-mile when he saw the riders cutting across the
slopes to head him off. He recognized Ken Dixon at the
head, counted some ten horsemen. He cut sharply to his
right, sent the pinto down a slow incline, and saw
Dixon slow as he caught sight of the line of pursuing
cavalry. Fargo watched the man take his band to the
left, swing in to keep after him, yet leave enough room
between him and the troopers.

Fargo raced the pinto up a slope, veered the horse to
the left, and moved toward Ken Dixon's pursuing riders.
He glanced back and saw the lieutenant send his column
in a sharp left, head his men almost directly at the
smaller band of pursuers. Fargo held his ground and
then swerved back to the right, in almost a forty-degree
turn. He smiled as he saw Richardson pull his men
around to give chase and he watched Dixon lead his

band forward, then turn to continue the chase. He turned, angled his way across a long, flat slope, his course giving Dixon's men an advantage, and he saw them spur their horses. He glanced back again to see Richardson veer toward them, slow his charge enough to let his men fire a quick volley of shots that made Dixon peel off.

Fargo swerved the pinto again, the other direction this time, and the cavalry platoon raced after him. He saw Dixon's men return to the pursuit but stay to his left. They both figured he was racing rabbitlike in a mindless attempt to flee, but with every swerve and cut, Fargo had moved forward in one steady direction, marking places he had fixed in his mind, and now he suddenly raced the pinto in a straight line, sending the horse full out. He saw the lieutenant bring his column up behind him, glanced around to find Ken Dixon staying on a parallel course, on land a few dozen yards higher, making better time than the troopers.

Both groups were watching him and each other, he saw, exactly as he'd expected they would. Neither saw the two Cheyenne sentries high in the rocks. Fargo, racing straight ahead, saw both Indians leap from their lookout posts and disappear from view. They would be at the main camp in minutes, he knew, sounding the alarm. All they could see was two war parties of white-eyes racing toward their camp, led by a lone horseman charging out in front of the rest.

Fargo saw Dixon's men pulling in closer, passing the troopers, and he caught the lieutenant's nervous glance at the smaller band of pursuers. The pinto raced into a sparse cover of maple and out the other side, and Fargo looked back to see the troopers closing in. He swept the higher ground. Dixon was moving down fast and Fargo sent the pinto racing along a flat stretch of ground. On one side, he saw the tree cover he'd used to get near the Cheyenne camp, but he charged straight ahead in open land. The broad pathway curved, became a plateau, and Fargo pulled back on the pinto, turned the horse as he came to a halt. He glanced back as Richardson and his men galloped around the curve and reined in sharply, kept watching as Dixon's band came into view only to pull to a halt. He glanced ahead where the Cheyenne stretched across the plateau in three rows. Near to a hundred warriors, he guessed, at least seventy-five. He heard the high-pitched, hooting scream, and the triple row of horsemen charged, splitting into three groups, one veering to come in from the right, the other the left, and one charging head-on.

Fargo spurred the pinto toward the trees, saw Richardson's face ashen with fright and surprise. Dixon's men had already started to mill in a tight circle, he saw. But it was too late to run, and as he raced into the trees, he saw the lieutenant start to deploy his troopers to repel attack in proper army-manual formation.

Fargo winced, saw the first fusillade of arrows bring down four men. A dozen Cheyenne were moving up to engage Dixon's men, he saw, and he wheeled the pinto in the maple grove as he spied the three Cheyenne coming after him. He fired one shot and saw one of the Indians topple from his horse. Fargo dived to the ground as three arrows whistled over his head, and he saw one of the Indian ponies charging at him. He rolled again and the horse clipped him along his leg, flipping him sideways. He had chance only to see the second Cheyenne poised almost over him, letting an arrow fly.

Fargo tried to roll as the arrow caught him through the shirtsleeve and he felt the shirt rip. He saw the shadow come over him first as the Cheyenne leaped from the saddle, managed to brace himself as the Indian landed on him. He took the blow, let himself go back with it, got a knee up, and sent the bronzed figure falling backward.

He caught the flash on the other side of him, whirled, saw the second Cheyenne diving at him. He got the Colt up in time to fire a single shot, saw the bullet crash into the man's naked abdomen, tearing a gaping hole that suddenly filled with entrails spilling out like so many worms from a box. The Indian's cry was hardly that, a gargled noise as he hit the ground, and Fargo twisted again as the third Cheyenne came at him, a heavy bone knife in one hand. The red man swung the weapon in a short arc and Fargo dropped under the blow, dived forward, slammed into the man at the knees. The Cheyenne half-somersaulted, came down on his shoulders. He tried to spin, but the Colt barked again and the Indian continued his somersault, backward this time. Fargo stepped over the still form and swung onto the pinto, peered past the trees. The lieutenant's men had broken, tried to flee. A few still fought, but the plateau was strewn with blue-uniformed figures. Fargo's eyes moved to the higher ground and saw Cheyenne warriors on foot, picking over the lifeless bodies of Dixon's band.

He heard the whoops and shouts of pursuit. Some of Richardson's troopers were still running. And still being pursued, he noticed with grimness. He heard shots, enough of them. A fair part of the lieutenant's men had managed to run for it. Not many would continue running, he knew, not from a Cheyenne pursuit. But Dixon and his killers littered the high land, and the list was still in the pinto's saddlebag, Fargo grunted. It wouldn't bring back the innocent families who'd been sacrificed to causes, but it was a kind of justice, a down payment on not forgetting that people counted too.

He flicked the chamber on the Colt, saw there was only one shell left. He started to reload when he felt the hairs on the back of his neck suddenly grow stiff, the cold touch of danger wash over him. He half-turned, had just enough time to see the Cheyenne, a half-dozen yards away, tall, clad only in loincloth and wrist gauntlet. The man had his bow drawn back to his chin and Fargo saw the blur as the arrow left the bowstring. He spun, felt the shaft hurtle into the small of his back, through the gun belt, the pain sharp as the arrowpoint penetrated his body. He felt it hit something in his spine, felt the sudden weakness come over him. He was falling through blackness, conscious only of hitting the ground.

Light came back to him. He had no idea how long it took to do so, but suddenly he was aware of light. He blinked, stayed motionless, and let his eyes find a focus point. The base of a maple took shape. He stared at it, made certain it stayed in place. He became aware of the silence, the still, empty silence that surrounded him. He pushed against the ground with both hands and felt the point stabbing in his back. He half-turned, reached behind himself, got his hand around the arrow. He pulled awkwardly, kept the shaft straight so it wouldn't break off. It pulled free on the third try. The tip was red with his blood; it had struck a nerve, but the gun belt had absorbed most of it, the hard leather saving him from death.

He rose, drew a deep breath. The Indian had left him for dead and Fargo's eyes went out past the trees to the open land. The silence was made of the dead strewn across the plateau. Fargo's eyes swept the scene, frowned. The pinto was gone. The Cheyenne had taken the horse. Not surprising, he grunted. The Ovaro would be a prize among prizes. Fargo moved from the maples out onto the plateau. The slain troopers had been stripped of knives, belts, watches, and brass buttons.

Fargo climbed up to the higher land where Dixon's men lay in grotesque lifelessness. He moved among the bodies, turned two over with his foot. Dixon wasn't one of them, he saw. Fargo glanced up, saw the day coming to an end. He walked down to the plateau again, followed it to the curve where at least some of Richardson's troopers had fled. He came on six more troopers slain, two scalped. He walked on another half-mile, found one more soldier. He made a quick count in his mind, came up with nineteen troopers. Nineteen out of twenty-five. Richardson had escaped with but six of his platoon left alive.

Fargo turned back to the plateau as the night started to slip across the land. The Cheyenne camp wasn't more than a half-mile beyond. He walked slowly, reached the camp as the night grew dark, dropped to one knee, and peered at the scene. Celebration bonfires, victory dances, a little Bingham-weed juice, the camp filled with chanting and laughter.

Fargo's eyes moved around the outer edges till he found the horses tethered together. He began to circle the camp, staying in the brush and trees, moving carefully, until he reached the horses. He spotted the Ovaro at once and swore under his breath. They'd taken the saddle from the horse, and he crept forward on hands and knees to the very edge of the camp circle. The flickering fires, mostly in the center of the camp, cast enough light for him to see the small pyramid of saddles, mostly army gear, stacked beside one of the tepees. In the morning they'd strip the saddles of anything they could use, leather for pouches and tepee flooring, cinch straps to use pulling travois, stirrups as decoration or coup prizes.

Fargo edged back a few paces and lay flat on the ground. It promised to be a long night, He half-dozed, listened to the sounds of dancing and singing finally die down and the big victory fires become heaps of hot ashes. He watched a half-dozen squaws file into the tepee next to the saddles and was grateful for small favors. He waited another hour until the camp became silent, the tepees closed, a half-dozen revelers passed out on the ground across the camp. He rose, moved into the camp on silent steps, stayed crouched, and dropped to one knee when he reached the saddles. He espied his midway down the pyramid and began to carefully lift the other saddles to the ground. He had just lifted the last one atop his when he caught the soft footsteps moving around the tepee. Fargo took the throwing knife from its leg holster and crouched low behind the remaining mound of saddles. He saw the Indian come into view, the man alert, his eyes scanning the saddles. Fargo watched as he frowned at the two piles of saddles, plainly trying to remember whether there had been two stacks or one. He watched, not daring to breathe, as the Indian continued to stare at the saddles. Slowly the

Cheyenne looked up from the two pyramids, his eyes narrowed as they peered past the tepee.

Shit, Fargo bit out silently. The Cheyenne sensed something was wrong. He wasn't sure, but he sensed it. The Indian stepped forward again and Fargo saw the tomahawk in his hand.

Silence was everything. One cry of alarm from the Cheyenne and there'd be no fleeing with horse and saddle, probably not with his life. He waited, let the man come closer, the Indian taking careful steps. Fargo's hand turned the knife upward and his powerful shoulder muscles grew tight. The Indian was almost to him. One more step would do it. Fargo forced down the urge to leap up, strike with the knife, and he felt the tiny beads of perspiration trickling down the side of his temple.

The Indian started the final step, came around the second pyramid of saddles, held for an instant as he saw the crouched figure before him, unable to push aside surprise. Fargo sprang up, the thin, double-edged blade held spearlike before him. He drove it through the Indian's jaw from the bottom, fastening his jaw clamped shut as the blade went into the roof of his mouth, not unlike a big pin.

Fargo caught the man as he started to collapse, kept the blade jammed hard through the Indian's jaw. The man's guttural sounds were all kept silently inside his clamped jaws. Still keeping the blade pressed hard up through the man's jaw, Fargo lowered the Cheyenne to the ground. Slowly he began to pull the blade out. The man's jaw came open and twin trickles of red started to seep from the corners of his mouth.

Fargo wiped the blade clean on the grass, returned it to its holster, and rose, lifted his saddle, and carried it to where the Ovaro restlessly moved on a long tether. The horse whinnied at once in greeting and Fargo put a hand on the soft snout, whispered soothingly to the horse. He put the saddle on, cut the tether, and had just finished tightening the cinch when he heard movement in the camp. He turned, saw the squaw that had just stepped from the tepee. She stared at the lifeless form on the ground beside the saddles.

Fargo vaulted onto the pinto just as she let out a wailing scream, a high-pitched, undulating sound that wobbled across the camp. He was racing into the night as he heard the half-awake shouts, the sounds of sudden commotion. He rode fast but not hard. They'd search the perimeters of the camp, but that was all. They were too tired with celebration and weed juices to do more, and he headed the pinto into the high land as dawn tinted the night sky.

He continued riding till the new day came full, found a shaded place by a patch of wild plums, and slid from the saddle. He slept heavily until the body let him wake and he saw the sun had gone past the noon sky. He washed with canteen water, ate of the wild plums, and finally halted beside his saddlebag. He stared at the leather pouch. It lay there, just a leather pouch, yet somehow malignant, an inanimate object made into throbbing evil by man. How many had died because of its contents? Too many, he growled. He would destroy it now. They had tried to kill him for it, but he had turned that against them. They were both alike. One more life sacrificed to the cause didn't matter. They were both possessed by their own righteousness. The wrong thing for the right reasons, he spit out as he swung onto the pinto. History was full of it, those who committed every sin in the good book under the excuse of a righteous cause. The pouch was a prize neither deserved and neither would have. He'd destroy it now, he echoed silently.

After he reached Amber. She could destroy it with him. She deserved that much. She had been used and they would have killed her if it had become necessary. She had to realize that now and know that her father had agreed. She hadn't been killed like the wagon-train families. They had killed only a part of her.

He rode on, not hurrying. There was no need for that anymore. But when he reached the balsams, he quickened the pinto's pace, headed down to the flatland below, and saw the ranch come into sight. He rode onto the ranchland, a quiet place now, the calves in the corrals but no hands at work. He halted at the house and glimpsed Amber's face at the window, her eyes round as she looked out at him.

He swung from the horse and she opened the door as he reached it, her eyes filled with pain in their amber depths. "I hoped you wouldn't come back," she said quietly, and he felt the frown pull at him as he stepped through the doorway.

"I told her you'd come here," he heard the voice say. His hand flashed downward, had the Colt half-out of the holster when the voice came again.

"Do it, and she gets it full in the back," it said.

Fargo froze, opened his fingers, and let the Colt fall back in the holster. He looked past Amber to see Ken Dixon step into view, the rifle in his hands, the barrel aimed at Amber's back. Fargo fastened blue-quartz eyes on the man.

"I got away," Dixon said. "Managed to hide till it

got dark. I came right here. Been waiting for you to show." Fargo saw the man's eyes grow small with hate. "You bastard. You suckered us into it."

Amber's voice cut in. "He made me go to the window so you'd see me," she said almost tearfully.

Ken Dixon's smile was a twisted grimace. "I told her you'd be back. It's your kind of gesture," the man said. His voice grew harsh. "Turn around," he ordered. Fargo obeyed and felt Dixon take the Colt out of its holster. "Turn around again," Dixon said, and Fargo faced him. The man rammed the rifle barrel into his stomach and Fargo doubled over with the sudden, sharp pain. "The list," Dixon rasped.

Fargo, still doubled over, squeezed words through pain-filled breath. "I tore it up," he said.

Dixon swung the rifle stock in a short, upward arc. It crashed into the side of the big man's face and he went down on one knee. "Don't bullshit me, you bastard," Dixon snarled.

Fargo looked up from one knee, measured the distance to the rifle. Too far, he saw. He'd be blasted before he took two steps. He pulled himself to his feet, his head throbbing. "Why would I keep it?" he asked.

Dixon answered with contempt. "For some stupid reason of your own," he said. "Outside. Let's see what you've got in your saddlebag."

He moved back, gestured to the door with the rifle, and Fargo stepped from the house, cursing inwardly. Dixon held the rifle steady, moved in a sideways walk to the pinto. "Stay right there," he ordered Fargo. He peered into the saddlebag, flicked his eyes to the big black-haired man, and drew the leather pouch from the saddlebag. His smile was made of ice. Fargo saw Amber standing near him, concern and fear in her face.

"Well, now, I think we're in business," Dixon said, flicked a glance quickly, and saw Fargo's eyes on the rifle. "Try it and I'll blow your gut apart," the man said.

Fargo stayed in place and Dixon kept his eyes riveted on him as he spoke to Amber. "Now, you bring those two horses around, little lady," the man said. Fargo watched her go behind the stable, reappear leading two saddled mounts. Dixon put the leather pouch inside the front of his shirt as he stepped toward Fargo. "You've some luck running for you. I'd like to blast you, but I've only a few bullets left. I can't waste them until I find some more," the man said. "So little Amber, here, is going with me." His eyes narrowed, his face taking on icy hardness. "You come after me, Fargo, I so much as see your shadow, and I'll blow her head off. You better believe me, mister," he said.

"I believe you," Fargo said grimly. It was no lie. The man would kill her without a second thought. The leather pouch was everything. Nothing counted except that.

Dixon studied him a moment longer. "I don't figure you, Fargo," he said. "The list doesn't mean a damn thing to you. You don't care about either side. All you had to do was turn it over to me or to the Yankees. Why didn't you?"

"You don't deserve it. Neither do they," Fargo said.

"Turn around," Dixon said disdainfully.

Fargo turned, met Amber's pain-filled eyes for a brief moment. The rifle stock crashed onto the back of his head. He felt only the moment of pain, and then nothing. He didn't even feel himself hit the ground.

He woke with his head pounding. He forced his eyes open, paused, pulled himself up to rest on his knees. He saw the house in front of him, the door hanging open. The day was growing long, the sun behind the hills, he saw, and he painfully got to his feet. His head continued to pound and felt sticky to the touch. He half-stumbled into the house, found a bucket of cold water, and washed caked blood from the bruise at the back of his head. His hand touched the empty holster and he swore silently. He dried himself and went outside. Dixon had his Colt but the big Sharps was in its saddle holster. The man had made one mistake. He had to sleep sometime. It would be just a matter of waiting.

And being so very careful, Fargo muttered as he climbed onto the horse. The man was ruthless and he'd be nervous. He'd be quick to shoot. One mistake and it'd mean Amber's life, Fargo realized He'd have to stay far back until the right time came. He picked up their trail without trouble, the two horses moving side by side. They had at least two hours' start, probably three. Fargo didn't push to catch up but contented himself with trailing their path.

He frowned as he saw the tracks move toward Hollowville as the day began to fade. He followed the tracks until the night blanketed the land, low clouds blotting out the moon. He settled down at a little rocky place to wait for the moon or morning. He dozed, slept a cat's sleep, and morning came first as the clouds stayed through the night. He rose, freshened his face with the canteen water, and picked up the trail again, his frown deepening. The tracks led to a lean-to shanty a half-mile outside Hollowville. When they continued on, there were three horses.

Fargo's mouth grew tight and he swore aloud. "Son of a bitch," he bit out as he began to trail the hoofprints again. He couldn't be certain yet, but he was damned unhappy. He stepped up his pace, but Dixon had traveled most of the night, little cups of dew in the hoofprints. It was late afternoon when he began to draw closer to the three horses, and he slowed, hung back plenty far enough. He let the day slip into dusk before he moved forward again, picking up the tracks as they led up into a small stand of serviceberry. He dismounted as the night came, moved forward on foot, and led the pinto behind him. He paused when he smelled coffee, draped the pinto's reins over a low branch, and crawled forward. He spotted the campsite, a fire hardly more than glowing embers, giving barely enough light. But he saw what he feared he'd see, and his lips pulled back in silent anger.

There'd be no waiting for Dixon to sleep, no biding time for the exact moment. Dixon had taken on a guard so he could sleep, and Fargo saw the man, his back against a tree, the rifle held upright in one hand. Dixon's threat to kill Amber had done its job, made him stay back far enough until the second man was picked up. It was simple now. Dixon and the other man would take turns staying on guard.

Fargo swore again as his eyes found Amber. She had her wrists tied, lay almost alongside Dixon, and he saw the man had his rifle barrel aimed at her as she slept. No way, Fargo muttered, not even with the throwing knife. The risk was too great, the chance of a mistake too final for Amber. Dixon had closed off his one chance.

Fargo crawled backward, moved away from the camp, inching his way, afraid of an unexpected loose stone, a dry twig that might snap. He was perspiring when he reached the pinto. He'd no way to get to the man now. Dixon left him no room for a mistake. And worst of all, the bastard knew he had the trump card. Fargo cursed the man's rotten cleverness as he climbed onto the pinto, turned the horse around.

Dixon held the trump card for only one reason and Fargo's brow furrowed as he rode. Dixon was moving south, his progress slow but steady. He had a long way to go yet, and it wouldn't be hard to pick up his trail. Fargo's mouth became a thin line as he sent the pinto into a fast canter. He had no choice. There was no guarantee he wouldn't do away with Amber when he was finished with her. When he had delivered that list, Amber might be more burden than help. There was no choice, Fargo muttered again as he settled down to hard riding.

He rested the horse twice during the night, once a little after dawn, and the sun was high as he raced past the bur oaks and down the road beyond. He saw the buckboard in front of the house as he rode up, two traveling bags in the rear compartment. Charles Dodson came out of the house as he reined to a halt and leaped from the saddle in one motion. The man's face was made of ice, but his eyes held surprise.

"Jody," Charles Dodson called, and Fargo saw the flash of new-wheat hair in the doorway. She came out looking entirely too attractive in a tan skirt and tan blouse. She stared at him in disbelief.

"Back to Washington?" Fargo commented.

"You've a nerve coming here," Charles Dodson said.

Jody almost echoed the severity in the old man's face. "What do you want? Haven't you done enough damage?" she snapped.

"Richardson make it back?" Fargo asked.

"Barely, with only six of his men left," Dodson said. "Though I fail to see why that concerns you."

"Not a guilty conscience, I'm sure," Jody said.

"Nope," Fargo agreed. He moved his eyes to Charles Dodson. "Dixon has the list," he said, and heard Jody gasp.

Charles Dodson's eyes took on new sharpness. "You know that as a fact?" he questioned.

"He took it from me," Fargo said.

"You taking sides, finally, Mister Fargo?" the man said.

"No," Fargo snapped back. "He's got Amber Holloway, too. He's holding her as a hostage. He'll kill her if I try to take him."

"And you won't risk that," Jody put it, the edge of waspishness in her voice.

"That's right. She never had any part of it. She's one

more innocent victim. I can't risk her life, and he knows it," Fargo said.

"Why'd you come here?" Charles Dodson asked sharply.

"You said Richardson has six men left. That's enough to take him," Fargo said.

"What about the girl's life?" the man questioned.

"A hostage is nothing if nobody cares. A hostage is only good if somebody cares about her or him," Fargo said. "He knows you won't give a damn about what happens to Amber Holloway." The man's silence answered the statement, and Fargo felt the grim smile touch his lips. "He'll know it like I know it. He can't use her as a hostage against you. She's useless to him for that. He'll have to run or go down fighting."

Charles Dodson's lips pursed and his eyes glittered with racing thoughts. "Why should we help you in this? Why should we give a damn about what happens to Amber Holloway?" the man speared.

"You know the answer to that," Fargo said. "You'll get the list."

The man peered at him, his eyes still glittering. "You'll never pick up his trail," Fargo said. "I can. I'll find him for you. You do the rest."

"We get the list, Fargo," Charles Dodson said. "No tricks from you. No running off with it." Fargo nodded. "Your word as a gentleman?" Dodson pressed.

"No running off with it. My word," Fargo said grimly.

"Get the lieutenant, Jody," Charles Dodson said. "I'll wait here."

Fargo leaned his big frame against the hitching post as Jody vanished behind the house. She reappeared on the gray mare, riding hard, and vanished down the road. Charles Dodson's eyes took in the big black-haired man. "You're going to have to choose sides one of these days, Fargo," he said.

"Maybe," Fargo allowed. "When the time comes. Not before. Not now. Maybe it'll never come."

"Oh, it will come," the man said, and Fargo caught the sudden sadness in his tone. "Things have gone too far now. I'm afraid there'll be no turning back. You'll be choosing."

"Sometimes a man doesn't do much choosing," Fargo said. "It just turns out he's in one place or another when the time comes. He doesn't choose his ideas. They grow up with him."

Charles Dodson's smile was appraising. "When the time comes, I hope it'll be our side," he said.

Fargo shrugged. It wasn't time for that and he'd seen precious little to choose between them so far. He kept his thoughts to himself. It didn't take too long when he heard the sound of horses moving fast along the road. He saw the lieutenant first, the six men behind him, still riding smartly in twos.

Richardson reined his horse to a halt in front of him, and Fargo saw the man's face red with anger. "I ought to shoot you right here and now," the man flung at him.

"You were going to kill me for that list, Lieutenant," Fargo said calmly. "I just saved my neck."

"You bastard," the lieutenant shouted at him.

Charles Dodson's calm voice cut in. "Lieutenant Richardson, we can't let personal animosities get in the way now. Fargo has brought us a golden opportunity, a last chance. And a chance to redeem himself." The man nodded. Fargo smiled back. "I'm going along this time," Dodson said.

"I can shoot damn well," Jody said.

Dodson shrugged. "Every gun will help," he agreed. He strode to the small stable behind the house, reappeared on an army mount. "We're ready, Mister Fargo," he said.

Fargo climbed onto the pinto and rode point. It was dusk when they reached the beginning of Dixon's trail and he followed the prints until night made it impossible. The lieutenant chose the campsite and Fargo took a spot off by himself. Jody bedded down near Charles, he saw. He let himself sleep quickly; the morning would bring a hard-riding day.

He set a fast pace until noon, then slowed, rested the horses, and crouched down to study the trail. By evening he'd found the third camp Dixon had made and he took note of the fact that the man chose a half-circle each time, one where his back was protected and it was easy to spot anyone approaching from three-quarters of the circle. Fargo bedded down off by himself again, had almost gone to sleep when he saw the new-wheat hair coming toward him. He sat up and Jody halted, knelt down in front of him.

"You doing all this just to save Amber Holloway?" she asked.

"That's a good reason," he said.

"It's a good reason. Is it your only one?" she prodded.

"I gave Charles my word," he said. "No running off with it at the last minute."

"I know you did. I just want to be sure you're going to keep it," Jody said.

"I'll keep it," he told her, and she tried to see behind his expressionless face, gave up, and rose to her feet.

"You're a strange man, Fargo," she said.

"Yep." He nodded.

"I'll remember you," she murmured.

"For all kinds of reasons." He grinned.

"Yes," she said thoughtfully. "For all kinds of reasons."

She turned and walked back to her bedroll. He watched her settle down, turned on his side, and slept.

The day came in under gray clouds and he picked up the trail again. Dixon had slowed somewhat and Fargo halted at a place where they'd rested the horses. He knelt down, ran his fingers along the long-bladed fescue grass. Most of the blades had gone back to an upright position. Most, but not all.

"They're not more than four hours ahead of us," he said, and returned to the saddle. He set a fast pace for nearly three hours, then slowed, studied the tracks that went into a tall-treed woodland terrain. He halted, let Richardson come up alongside him, and pointed to the tracks on the ground. "I'm dropping back. You trail point from here on. If you go wrong, I'll catch it," he said.

"I won't go wrong," Richardson said stiffly.

Fargo grunted. "It's important that Dixon see you," he said. "So keep on pushing forward. Don't try to sneak up on him." His glance went to Charles Dodson. "When he sees you, he'll have to make a quick decision, try to run or fight."

"What do you expect?" Dodson asked.

"I think he's tired by now. There's only so far a man can run. He'll see there's only seven troopers. I say he'll put up a fight, try to get as many as he can," Fargo answered.

"Where will you be then?" the lieutenant asked with an edge in his voice. "Can we count on you for help?"

"Soon as he's concentrating on you and not Amber, I'll be there," Fargo said cheerfully. He held the pinto still as the lieutenant moved forward.

Jody passed him and he saw her eyes on him, apprehension in their misty depths. He tossed her a smile and stayed back. He rode slowly, kept Jody and Dodson just in sight as they drew up at the rear of the column. The afternoon had started to slide toward an end when he saw the riders halt, heard Richardson bark orders.

Fargo jumped down from the pinto and ran on foot alongside the column, dropped to a crouch. They'd caught sight of Dixon and the man had seen them in return. Fargo crept forward, stayed in the bushes. He saw Dixon and the other man, both crouched behind a fallen log, one at each end. His eyes scanned the area and he spotted Amber, her wrists still tied. Dixon had her against the trunk of an oak, to one side.

Fargo stayed hidden, watched as Richardson sent his horse closer, his six troopers moving behind him.

"We want the list, Dixon," Fargo heard the lieutenant call. "Give us the list and you can walk away alive."

"Come get it, Yankee," Dixon called back.

"You're outnumbered," Richardson returned. "Give us the list."

"I've Amber Holloway here. I'll kill her if you come for me," Dixon said.

"You know that means nothing to us, Dixon," Fargo heard Richardson say. He nodded inwardly. It was the right answer. All too goddamned true, too, and Dixon knew that.

Fargo saw Richardson start forward again. The shot exploded, blew the lieutenant's hat off as he ducked down. Fargo started to move back, rose, ran to the pinto. He heard the lieutenant's command barked out, glimpsed the troopers charge forward. The gunfire exploded at once, filling the forest with sound and the sharp smell of gunpowder. Dixon and the other man were laying down a good barrage and he saw two troopers go down. Richardson was charging, three troopers spreading out behind him. Fargo raced the pinto through the trees on the other side where Amber lay. He neared the battle scene, saw Dixon's man draped lifelessly across the one end of the log. He vaulted from the pinto as he saw Amber trying to dig herself into a row of bushes. He slid on his knees to her, used the double-edged blade to slice through her wrist bonds. She stared at him, relief, surprise, fear all in her eyes.

"Stay here," he said, rose, and swung onto the pinto. He saw Dodson and Jody coming up and to the right, Richardson and two of his troopers on foot. Dixon had tried to race into the heavier brush and Fargo saw the man's figure stumble, fall as rifle fire poured into him. He saw two shots slam into Dixon's back, another into his left leg. The man turned, tried to bring his rifle up to fire, but a shot shattered the side of his head. Dixon fell back to land half-sitting against the base of a tree.

Fargo pulled the Sharps out, brought it to his shoulder. He fired three rounds into Ken Dixon's chest. "Cease firing. He's dead," the lieutenant shouted, and Fargo lowered his weapon. He moved forward with the others to stare down at the lifeless figure.

"The list, get the list," Charles Dodson said, and Richardson knelt beside the man, started to go through his pockets.

"Check his saddlebag," Richardson ordered, and one of the troopers hurried to find the horse.

"Not in here," Fargo heard the man call after a moment.

"He doesn't have it," Richardson said, getting to his feet. Fargo felt Dodson's eyes on him.

"Did you trick us into this, Fargo?" the man asked.

Fargo slipped from the pinto and walked to Ken Dixon's shattered body. He ripped the man's shirt open. "He was carrying it here when I saw him last," he said. He saw the leather pouch, now more red than tan, pulled it out. He opened the thong, shook the contents out onto the ground. Little pieces of torn, blood-drenched paper fluttered to the ground like so many strange leaves.

Richardson pushed at them as they lay on the ground. "They are ruined. You can't read anything on them," he said. "Nothing's left of them."

Fargo stood up, met Charles Dodson's piercing eyes. He shrugged. "I gave you my word. No running off with it," he said.

Dodson's eyes stayed on him, the man's face severe. Fargo shrugged again and he watched Charles Dodson slowly nod. "I hope you'll choose our side when the time comes, Fargo," the man said.

"Give my regards to the President," Fargo said as the man moved his horse slowly past. He watched Richardson and the others gather up the wounded men. Jody moved past him.

"Bastard," she said softly, not looking at him.

He stayed in place, watched the others move on, turning back out of the trees, and he saw Amber standing very still, her eyes on him. He started toward her and she half-ran, half-fell into his arms. He sank down on the ground with her, held her until she stopped shuddering. "What now?" she asked.

"I don't know about you, but I was hired to take a wagon train of hides through Cheyenne country. That's what I'm going to do," he said.

She blinked at him, her amber eyes grave. "Yes, that sounds like a perfect idea," she said slowly.

"It's going to be a slow trip," he said, and she questioned with her eyes. "I expect to do as much screwing as scouting," he said.

"That sounds even more perfect," she said as he pulled her to her feet. "Let's hurry back and get those wagons."

He nodded. He'd take the Cheyenne over causes any day.

LOOKING FORWARD!

The following is the opening section
from the next novel
in the exciting new
Trailsman series from Signet:

The Trailsman #19:
SPOON RIVER STUD

The early 1860s—Spoon River,
a town in the Dakota Territory,
where strong men live by the gun
or die by it.

Three days of hard riding had left Fargo almost too tired
to sleep. His nerves were frayed from forcing himself
too far, too long. He needed a good sound sleep, the
kind that gives a man back body and mind.

For the last hour the sun pounded on him like a ham-
mer, and now at last he was hit with sudden drowsiness.
The lake-blue eyes in the bronzed square face slid almost
shut. He had stopped hours ago at the saloon in Spoon
River and the one shot of bourbon hadn't helped keep
him alert. He stared at a great spreading oak with a

thick trunk stuck in the earth; its cool shade beckoned him. He mopped his neck; the intense heat even hit his loins, and his body seethed. He cursed, nudged the sweating Ovaro to the oak, and when he reached the shade, his big, lean, muscled body slipped off the horse. He crawled on the cool carpeted grass to the trunk, leaned against it, shut his eyes, and was asleep in moments.

Only a minute it seemed could have passed when he felt himself snap awake. He wasn't alone, and he felt a sudden kick against his boot.

"Hey!" A woman's voice, throaty, sexy. Slowly his eyes focused on her. The kick came again.

"Looks like a live one," a voice said.

His eyes now fully open, he found himself staring at three women. The three women each held a gun. No damn little dance-hall pistols, but real six-guns.

He shut his eyes, then opened them, expecting the women would be gone. But they weren't, and they weren't smiling either. The blond woman nearest, the one who kicked his boot, had cobalt-blue eyes, and the gun she held was rock-steady. There were two good-looking women behind her, and they didn't look friendly either. But they did look familiar.

"What's the name, cowboy?" the blonde asked.

He started to get up.

"Don't move till I tell you," she said sharply.

He stared into her blue eyes, and they looked deadly serious. She had a saucy, long-lipped mouth, a pert, pretty face, and wore, as did the others, tailored riding breeches, a checked shirt, and fine leather boots.

"The name is Skye Fargo. And don't get nervous. You've got three guns."

She nodded. "And you won't look good with three holes. Get his gun, Maude."

Maude, a redhead with white skin and a fine expanse of chest, bent toward his right holster. He was ready to make a lightning grab, use the redhead for cover, pull his gun, but the blonde, watching like a hawk, did some thought reading.

"No tricks, Fargo, or you're already gone."

He smiled slowly. She was fast, a gun-smart filly, but he didn't like finding himself looking into her gun like this. Still, he was eaten up with curiosity: what in hell did they want with him? Money, guns, the horse? They didn't seem to need such things: they looked well-fed, well-cared-for, respectable, even prosperous.

Maude, the redhead, flung his gun into a cluster of bushes, and then she and the other woman, a black-eyed brunette, holstered their guns.

Now they looked him over, every inch of his body, it seemed, the way you'd look at a horse before you bought it. Would they look at his teeth, too? he wondered.

He, in turn, stared back, but that didn't faze them one bit. Suddenly it hit him why they looked familiar. He'd seen the redhead and the brunette in the general store that very morning in Spoon River. Just a glimpse, for he'd been in a hurry, but he remembered they were both well-shaped and looked like respectable married women.

The blonde moved her gun slightly and it was now pointed, he was aware, directly toward his heart.

"What's the gun for, honey?"

"To keep you well-behaved. And the name is Abigail."

"I'll behave," he said.

Again the silence and the looking.

"Are you going to buy me?" he asked suddenly.

Abigail's eyebrows rose sharply. "Why'd you say that?"

"You're looking at me like I'm a slab of meat."

Abigail grimaced. "In a way, Fargo, you are." She turned to the brunette. "Give him some whiskey, Julia."

Julia walked to the horses grazing under a nearby maple, took a bottle and a tin cup from the saddlebag. When she gave him the cup, it was almost half-full.

"Not a bad idea." He gulped down some of it.

"Drink it all," Abigail commanded.

"Why not?" He grinned. It was all friendly enough, and it seemed she wasn't going to shoot him after all.

"Give him another."

He looked at Julia while she poured again—glowing black eyes in a face that was pretty but a bit hard. She studied him without smiling, then started toward the horses, joined by Maude.

He sipped the drink.

"Drink it all," Abigail said.

He gazed at her. "So that's your evil game?"

She frowned. "What?"

"You trailed me, woke me, stole my gun. All this to get me drunk."

She smiled. "No, Fargo. I want you to have a few drinks to cushion the shock."

He scowled. "Shock? What shock?" There was no way of figuring this woman. Was she going to shoot him for kicks after all?

Her smile stayed fixed, as though it were painted on. "Fargo, you're a lucky man. We're going to give you the privilege of having a tumble with two lovely women." She jerked her thumb at Maude and Julia.

Fargo stared. She might be smiling, but she seemed dead serious.

"Give me that again?"

Her eyes never wavered. "I think you heard me."

He spoke slowly. "You mean, you did all this—threatened to shoot, stole my gun, pumped me with liquor—to force me to tumble those two ladies?"

"Yes, I suppose I did." Her tone was level.

He stroked his chin. She had an upturned nose, a saucy mouth, and under those tailored riding pants, a damned shapely body. If he had to tumble someone, she'd have been his first choice.

"Why didn't you just ask politely?" he said.

She leaned forward as if she didn't get it. "What?"

"If you wanted me to bed the ladies, why didn't you just ask me?" He glanced about, saw only Julia with the horses. Where was the other?

Abigail squinted. "Are you trying to trick me, Fargo? Because if you are, you won't get away with it."

He shook his head. "I'm more than happy to oblige the ladies." He grinned. "I was never in a better mood for it."

Her face was grim as she studied him. "You mean it, don't you? You don't mind playing stud?"

That hit him wrong, somehow. "Playing stud" sounded as though it were something low-down. He didn't like it, but pushed the thought out of his mind. Instead he remembered that he hadn't had a woman for a week, that he'd been horny as a goat. And that the booze was already buzzing in his veins.

"The truth is, Abigail, I feel like a sex-starved stallion."

Her mouth twisted, and her smile was not nice. "Men

always brag about their sex powers, don't they, Fargo?"
She pointed behind him. About two hundred feet away
there was a hedge of bushes about ten feet high, a neat
hideaway most likely. "Go there. You'll find Maude
waiting. See if she likes stallions."

Fargo stared at her. She was one damned peculiar
filly. "Tell me, these ladies could get any man just by
whistling, just why are they doing this?"

Her face hardened. She had a look like steel under
silk. "That, Fargo, is none of your damn business. And
you're not to ask them. Just do it."

He nodded. He liked the way she fenced his questions,
the mocking smile, the saucy mouth, the round thrust of
her breasts, the way she handled herself. "Are you sure
you don't want to jump in this game? I'm ready when
you are."

The direct blue eyes drilled right through him. "That
will be the day, cowboy." Her hard tone jolted him,
and he wondered if she were angry at the sex game the
other ladies were playing. Did she work for them? He
wondered. Did she have a yen to get into the act, but
was fighting it? He threw that idea away as something
he'd like to believe. He glanced at the hedges and
pictured the redhead already there, ready for play. His
body responded. He stood and the bulge in his britches
couldn't help but catch her eye. But she maintained her
nice control.

"Just a minute, Fargo. This is a one-shot thing. After
it's over, you just keep riding, you understand? It will
be finished for all time."

His smile was cool; nothing, he thought, is ever
finished for all time.

He started toward the hedges, his loins loaded for

action. But there was still a burr at the back of his brain. He glanced over at Abigail; she still held the gun, her face unsmiling. Julia, watching them from near the horses, also kept her hand near her holster. As he walked, he felt strongly aware of their hard eyes, observing him, and then came the sting of anger. This was force, and he didn't like it. He had tried a checkmate, turning what they wanted at the point of a gun into an act of fun. He tried to make it a game, but they kept pushing, and he didn't like to be pushed—in anything.

The anger squelched desire, and by the time he went behind the hedges, the commotion in his britches had subsided.

Still, the sight of Maude jolted him. She had spread a bedroll on the grass and was sitting on it. She wore a silky chemise that revealed most of her breasts, nicely sized, her thighs and legs milk-white and shapely. Her red hair was knotted behind her head and she had blue-green eyes and full, sensuous lips. A sexy piece, all right. But still he felt the anger.

She glanced up at him. "Hurry, cowboy. Get your clothes off. You've got a hard day ahead."

He cocked his head. "You're not a bad-looking woman."

She scowled. "I'm not interested in your opinion. Don't waste time."

His jaw clamped. She was pretty bitchy—would that put an added edge to the action? He bent to his boots. "Try to be womanly. I'd like that better."

Her lips twisted almost in a sneer. "I don't give a damn what you like. We're not having an affair."

"What are we having?"

"Just a fast roll. Hurry and get this over with."

He scowled. She had about as much charm as a warthog.

He pulled his shirt off. "You've got lousy manners, Maude."

She stared back, as though in shock. "Who the hell do you think you are, cowboy? We grab you off the trail, offer you a shot any man would give his right arm for, and you talk about manners. Just do what you're supposed to and get the hell off."

Fargo grimaced. She was so nasty he felt coming on the kind of sex that had to have a core of anger. The thought hit him that the only way to get any pleasure out of this bitch was to lash her tail and then screw her silly. He pulled off his jeans and then his underpants.

She studied him with interest. "You look like you're pretty big, but I don't see any excitement there."

His smile was cold. "To tell you the truth, Maude, I don't see anything exciting here either."

She flushed and her eyes narrowed. Then she slipped off her chemise. She had a damned shapely body, fine shoulders, firm breasts with brown nipples, a soft rounded belly, full hips, and red fuzz over her triangle. He felt a quick shot of desire, but made no effort to encourage it. He'd rather not cooperate with this one.

"You've got a good body, Maude, but I'll tell you, honestly, something about being forced puts me off."

She scowled. "Well, mister, you better put it up or we may have to put you down."

He grinned. Yes, the only way—to bang hell out of the bitch. Make her work for it, and then pay her off.

"I wonder, honey, if it's possible to rape a man? There should be a way of starting it." He stepped in front of her.

Her blue-green eyes glittered with anger, but she stared at his maleness, which now hung heavy with the promise of power. Her breathing quickened, and as if aware there could be a lot of excitement here if she played his game, she flashed him a sullen look, then dropped between his knees. She took hold of him, pressed her face against him; then, stirred by awakening passion, she kissed and caressed him. Then, in a sudden surge of excitement, her mouth began a frenzy of movement. It went on and on, and he had to give in to the sheer pleasure in watching. She suddenly stopped, looked at his pulsating potency, and then said, "You see how easy it is to rape a man?"

She slid back on the bedroll, her legs spread apart, and looked up at him. He felt hard now with lust and there was just one way to go. He'd shaft her until she hollered uncle.

He crawled nimbly over her body, grabbed her breasts, touched the already erect nipples, but he didn't waste a moment with tenderness. He slipped quickly into the red fuzz mat to the inner warmth, thrusting firmly so that he went in all the way, and then heard the sharp intake of her breath. He was very large and she was nice and tight against his flesh; she felt it, too, for she began to squirm and groan. He began slowly, then went fast, and because she'd been so bitchy, he thrust his body against her hard, grabbing her silky butt with his strong hands, then pounding, making it a punishing kind of sex. This was how to do it, all right. The lady wanted sex, well, he'd give it to her in spades. He could hear her sharp gasps, her little squeals, her groans, and he knew it all sounded wild, but it was hard to tell whether it was pain or pleasure she felt. But he couldn't stop now. He felt her fingers gripping his back, the nails cutting into his flesh, and the pulling infuriated him. He thrust more violently, felt the great surge and anguish as he went into climax. As for her, poor thing, she lay squirming from side to side, hissing through her clenched teeth, as if he had violated her with an ax in addition to his mighty maleness.

He smiled grimly. She had wanted force; well, he'd given it. And, honestly, for him it had been a great ride.

He looked down at her red, flushed face, expecting to see anger, fury, expecting a tigress to rip back at him. But her damned face was now even radiant, her eyes looked starry. Son of a bitch, he thought, when it comes to sex, you can't match a woman. You think you're beating them to death, and instead, you're booting them into paradise!

Fargo was alone, behind the hedges, when he caught the strong smell of frying rabbit. He'd been thinking about Maude, who in spite of herself, had gone hellbent-for-heaven. Then he heard Abigail call out.

"Fargo! We've got some food. Come out."

He realized he had been sensing pangs of hunger. He slipped into his pants and grinned; they wanted to keep the stud well-fed so he could do the job properly.

Abigail's blue eyes glittered at him. She's trying to read me, to see if I liked it or hated it, he thought. She's a dilly.

Obviously not a trusting woman, she still held the gun and used it to point toward the meat now crispy brown in the frying pan. A pot of coffee simmered over the fire.

"To keep up your strength." Her mouth twisted with amusement.

"Yes, sex does leave a man hungry." He sat opposite her, dug into the meat, and chewed it with enjoyment. She watched, eyes alert, her face a mask. About a hundred feet away, Maude and Julia were in a huddle near the horses.

He said nothing until he cleaned off his plate and started on the coffee.

"What's your tie-in with these ladies?"

"Tie-in?" She smiled. "I'm the top gun, that's the tie-in."

He grinned. The chippie had a helluva confidence, and it wouldn't surprise him one damned bit if she could sharpshoot with the best. "I'm sure you can shoot the hair off a gnat's nose. But I mean something else."

"What do you mean, Fargo?"

"The women here want a party. Why are you left out?"

She smiled insolently. "I've told you. I don't want a party."

He stayed with it. "But don't you feel left out?"

She stared coldly, didn't even answer.

He shook his head. "It's one big puzzle."

Her lip curled. "Don't bother your head about it, Fargo."

He sensed a slithering movement ten feet from her. "Who shot the rabbit?" he asked casually.

Her saucy mouth smiled. "I did."

"Good." His tone was still casual. "You'll have to shoot a reptile ten feet to your left."

The blue eyes stared hard at him. "A trick, Fargo?" But she'd been alerted, and when the slithering started again, she fired. The snake, brown and thick, at least five feet long, jumped up, curling in agony, then went still. Its black small eyes still looked deadly.

"Son of a bitch!" she said. Then her face went soft. "Thanks, Fargo."

He lifted his coffeecup. "You're not a bad shot," he said.

She looked at the snake with distaste, turned to signal the startled women with the horses that all was well.

"Why do you want me to keep riding afterward?" he asked.

"It will be a lot healthier." Her pert face went grim.

"I'm not sure of that."

"What do you mean?"

"Facing two sex-hungry women can be more dangerous than facing anything else."

She shrugged and her gaze traveled over his body, lingering at the bulge in his britches. "Somehow, Fargo, I think you won't go down in defeat." She pointed her gun. "Now that you're rejuvenated, you can go back."

Again Fargo felt the sting of anger. In spite of joking, and the rambunctious kick he got from his romp with Maude, he didn't like force. He liked to pick his target, and he didn't like to be pushed to perform like a stud. He glanced at the plate as a weapon for diversion.

"Fargo!" The soft female voice had an edge of iron. "No tricks." Then her tone softened. "Just do your job, and you'll get out of this with your skin whole." She watched him stand, his eyes glittering. "After all, lying with a beautiful woman is a lot better than lying in a cold, lonely grave."

He scowled. "If you don't choose the woman, it's not that much better."

He still smoldered as he walked back behind the hedges. Julia sat there in a pink chemise, with a bottle in her hand, and she looked a touch soused.

She was almost plump with heavy breasts, nipples that stuck against the silk of the chemise. She had a well-shaped nose, a full lower lip, liquid black eyes, and sleek black hair that framed her milk-white skin. Her pretty face was frowning, as if she too didn't really go for this odd situation. But something about her still looked interested. She didn't come at him like Maude, ready to slug. Even looked a touch embarrassed. She poured a drink, gulped it. He grinned. Nothing whorish here; it was as though it were a strange experience; it might even be the first time she had tried it with a stranger passing through.

"I suppose we ought to hurry and get it over with." She lifted her chemise. She had a soft, rounded tummy and a luxurious patch of black hair between her thighs.

He smiled. "Hurry won't do a thing for pleasure, Julia."

She grimaced. "I don't think I'm supposed to be doing this for pleasure."

"What are you doing it for?" he asked quickly. She was half-soused and might spring the real reason.

Her lids fluttered over her black eyes. She had a touch of modesty, and he felt good about her for that.

"I can't tell you. Let's just go ahead. There isn't much time."

He slipped off his clothes, and as she waited, she took another generous swallow.

When he peeled off his britches, her eyes stared at him, fascinated. She had ticked off the right feelings and he knew how aroused he looked to her. He moved quickly, put his arms around her, and at the very touch of his flesh against hers, her breathing instantly quickened. She sat waiting, a pliant woman. He kissed her full lips, kept at it, and soon her mouth responded. He took her hand, put it over his throbbing rod of excitement. She pulled away as though it were a hot iron. He brought her back, and within moments she held him so hard it almost hurt; her mouth started to work against his lips.

His finger went down to her triangle and he stroked it, at first gently, then pushing into the lush, liquid warmth. She was hit by a great surge of passion and her mouth dropped open.

He let the fires build, then dropped to her breasts, stroked the nipple of each with his tongue. He caressed her curved voluptuous body, feeling the contours of her buttocks. And, along with all the rest, he kept moving his finger. She went limp with desire and they went down together to the bedroll, her face moving instantly close to his organ of excitement. She went for it with a natural appetite and made guttural sounds of pleasure. He felt a series of erotic waves, then slipped over her body, eased his bigness into her. He started slowly, but quickly reached a pitch of passion and began to pummel her, moving in and out, his hands holding on to her buttocks. Her curved smooth body gave him intense pleasure, and he kept thrusting, coming almost out, driving in, feeling her body rising in rhythm. It went on and on, and he glanced down to see her suffering agonies of joy. He drove harder, then his body tightened and he mobilized and exploded; she, too, went off, groaning like an animal in pain, flinging herself against his body, holding him with a deadly grip.

Excerpt from SPOON RIVER STUD

He stayed with her a short while; then, as he started to rise, her hands went out, as if to hold him longer.

He looked down at her white body with its plump breasts and tangle of dark hair at her pubis; her thighs were still trembling. She raised her eyes, and there was a strange expression in their blackness.

"Fargo, you bastard. I should never have done this." She looked away, her face tense. "It won't ever be this good again for me."

Much later, Fargo watched Maude and Julia mount their horses and start off in a canter toward Spoon River. Meanwhile Abigail swung over her gelding, still holding her gun, but her voice was friendly.

"Be smart, Fargo. Don't follow. Just keep on riding." Her blue eyes glinted strangely. "I think you gave much more than was expected. I'm sure the ladies were grateful. Good-bye and good luck."

She spurred the horse, which shot into a full gallop. She rode smooth as cream. He watched until she disappeared around a turn of trees and then smiled. She was a ding-a-ling, and easily the sweetest honey of them all. The one who got away. But you don't get everything you want in this world. Well, he'd go on now to Devil's Crossing, the place where he had been heading, trying to run down a lead on the low-down skunk he'd been tracking for vengeance.

He scoured the bushes for his gun, and when he found it, he gave it a thorough cleaning. The pinto had been grazing in a rich patch of grass. Fargo brushed and coddled him, then swung into the saddle. For one long moment he was tempted to turn east to Spoon River. Three beautiful women. It was intriguing. What made them do it? What was it all about? There were answers in Spoon River. But maybe it was better not to find them.

After all, he didn't exactly hate what had happened, did he?

He shrugged it off and turned the pinto west.

After a few hours' riding, he camped for the night near a small stream. He watched a quarter moon slowly climb while his beans and beef jerky heated over a fire in a dug pit. It never paid to advertise your whereabouts in this wild country, he thought, where man and animal, even man and man, preyed on each other. Still, the smell of frying beef drifted out and a coyote began to skulk around the edge of the camp. As he bit into the beef, he noted the Ovaro was chafing nervously. It's a hungry bitch of a coyote, he thought, and flung a couple of stones. The animal ducked and crept around until Fargo, aware it would be a bad night, regretfully pulled his gun, and at the next sight of the glittering eyes, drilled a hole between them. After that, the pinto went quiet, as did the night, that is, everything but his dreams, which, in spite of his recent sackful of sex, still continued erotic.

Curiously he dreamed not of the women he had lain with but the one he did not, the irresistible Abigail. In his dream she tossed her gun away and told him that, since he was such a pistol, she, too, wouldn't mind a tumble. He started to her, but she slipped away, behind the hedges, and hard as he looked, he couldn't find her. She had teased him, he thought, which left him furious. He was thrashing through the hedges when he was awakened by the shrill cry of a hawk that had just speared its prey. It was now daylight.

As he sipped hot coffee from his tin cup and meditated on the dream, he knew that the one woman who had truly reached him was the one he never caught. He thought about it as the pinto cantered west, and realized his urge to go back to Spoon River came not only from a desire to solve the mystery of the women, but also because Abigail was an unfinished story. Not only was she as pert a piece as he'd ever seen, but she was smart, sharp, and gun-wise.

He sighed, tried to put her out of his mind, and focused instead on the world around him. Now the sun hit the earth gently and the grass and flowers gleamed with rich midsummer color. Ahead of him, the golden rays turned the great range of mountains to the west into a massive bronze monument of stone.

The pinto moved at a leisurely pace, its great muscles rippling smoothly, and Fargo felt a sudden lightness, a stab of pleasure; it was a feeling that came often when he drifted out of the towns of men, a man alone on the trail, depending on his own skills to survive in a world of danger.

It was in this mood, looking at a stone shaped like a pike pointing toward heaven, when a shiver went through him. It was so slight a feeling that if he had not been trained long ago to stay alert to such signals from deep in his primitive alarm system, he would have bypassed it. But he didn't, he never did. Yet there was nothing about that even hinted danger. He turned the pinto toward a mass of rock, piled on each other, climbing at least five hundred feet. He felt his body go tense in the saddle. Still, he could see nothing. At the rocks, he started to climb, and after a hundred feet up, he worked more carefully, for movement was the great betrayer. When he got to a commanding view of the terrain, he stepped into a crevice and studied the land below.

Three riders were racing down a slope hellbent on something or someone.

The men looked tough, with short-brimmed black hats, leather vests, and each holstered two guns. Gunslingers on a hunt. But who was the quarry? They came to a halt and studied tracks. Whose? His tracks were the freshest. Could he be the quarry? But why? In Spoon River he had stopped just for supplies, and a fast lousy whiskey at Denny's Saloon. No trouble there. Of course, they could be blood kin to men he had killed in the past, deeds regrettable but unavoidable when a man was entitled to seek revenge. Not likely, in this case. These men sure looked ready for a killing. He was able to smell that sort of thing.

He watched and remembered that near a certain rock cluster, he had turned sharp off the trail to follow the tracks of a possum, which after a half-mile crisscrossed the track of coyotes, also interested in lunch. At that point, he swung back to the trail.

The riders shortly reached the rock clusters, stopped, followed his tracks to swing back on the trail. His jaw hardened: they were after him and he didn't have much time.

A quarter-mile west, scattered boulders looked like a good place to take cover. He came down the crags with care, hit the ground, then moved at high speed, putting the pinto into a hard run. They were three, and he was one; to equalize this, he needed surprise.

When he reached the boulders, he tethered the pinto out of sight, pulled his Colt, and settled down to wait.

Minutes dragged. His boot scuffed the earth and a gray mouse with bold, beady eyes stuck his nose out of a hole, curious to know who was invading his domain. The mouse streaked back. He smiled. Everyone has his own territory.

He waited and felt the heat of a hard sun hit the hand that cradled his gun. He had good position behind the boulder, and visibility of the trail for two hundred feet.

Then he heard the drumbeat of hooves against the earth, and he saw the riders coming in a file at a fast canter.

He put a bullet in front of the first horse, a sorrel, which snorted, pawed at the sky as the rider pulled hard on the bridle.

"Hold it right there," he called. The rider of the sorrel had a narrow cruel face with mean eyes, a vicious scar on his jaw. The riders behind also pulled up, their horses twisting and snorting at the hard bridling. The second rider had wild eyes and a red bandanna on his neck; the third rider looked very young, as if he didn't quite belong with such hard characters.

Fargo came out, gun in hand. "No wrong moves," he advised.

Scarface stared, his dark eyes taking in Fargo's face and body. Fargo smiled, as though friendly, and said, "Where you pilgrims heading?"

Scarface scowled. Not a man who justified his moves; gunslingers usually didn't, Fargo thought.

"What the hell difference does it make to you? We're just riding. It's a free country."

"Makes a difference," Fargo said. "Where you from?"

Scarface scowled. "Why'd you shoot at my horse?"

Fargo nodded pleasantly. "I thought it might be nice to have a little talk. Where you from?"

Scarface looked grim. "Spoon River." He paused. "You're pretty nervy, cowpoke. You're one gun. We're three guns. You're not talking smart for a man who likes living."

Fargo grinned. "Just keep in mind that if anybody here stops living, it won't be me."

The dark eyes in the narrow face slitted. He took slow, careful measure of Fargo.

"Listen, mister," he said, a crafty look in his eye. "We're on our way to Devil's Crossing. We got no quarrel with you. Don't even know who you are. We want no trouble."

Fargo studied him. The second rider, the one with the wild blue eyes, for the last minute had been inching his hand to his holster. Fargo seemed not to look at him.

"No, maybe you don't know me. My name is Fargo. And I don't want any trouble."

Just as he might have expected, his name triggered the nerves of the man with the wild eyes who itched to be a hero; he went for his gun. Fargo drilled a bullet into his forehead that blew the back of his skull off. He dropped from his horse in slow motion, crashing to the ground, where he fell facedown, his blood bubbling in the wound.

The horses stamped, but the riders froze, staring at their fallen comrade. Although Scarface was jolted, he made a quick recovery. "You had no call to do that,

Fargo." His voice was deadly guttural, his eyes small black pits.

"Your pal went for his gun," Fargo said easily. "Didn't care for my name, I reckon."

There was a moment of silence. "All we wanted, mister, was to get going," said Scarface. "We didn't want no trouble like that."

Fargo nodded grimly. "Then tell me, why were you tracking me?"

Scarface's eyes widened, but he handled it coolly. He shook his head, his face all innocence. "I swear you got it dead wrong. We were looking at tracks, yes, but we were tracking food. We followed a possum. No, you're wrong, Fargo, we had no quarrel with you. All we want now is to be on our way to Devil's Crossing and take this man home."

Fargo nodded, scratched his cheek, apparently convinced. He slipped his gun into the holster. "I guess I made a mistake. I'm sorry about your friend. He moved too quick. Go ahead, then."

And then again, just as Fargo sensed, Scarface made his move. It was fast. His gun was out of the holster, but before that, Fargo hit him twice in the chest. He catapulted back, fell off his horse, squirming, his heart spouting blood like a faucet. The third rider used the shooting time to drive his horse directly at Fargo, bringing up his gun. Fargo spun to his right as he fired, hitting the younger man's chest. He fell forward, got caught in the stirrup, and was dragged past Fargo. It took a fast leap to catch the bridle and bring the horse to a stop. He eased the man from the saddle to the ground, loosened his bloody shirt. He was indeed young, with pink cheeks, a soft mouth, and brown eyes clouded with pain.

Fargo felt a stab of pity, a kid cut off before he had lived because he mixed with the wrong men. "How'd you get tied up with these killers?" he asked, cradling the young man's head.

The brown eyes looked up, pain in them. "My brother."

His breathing came hard. He'd be gone in a minute. The blood leaked from his chest. The look of death was in his eyes.

"Who sent you after me, boy?"

The eyes stared dully. He was slipping away. His eyes were going empty. He was taking the secret with him.

Fargo's teeth clenched. He leaned to the man's ear. "Who?" he tried again.

The eyes were open, empty, he was dead.

Then suddenly the lips moved, whispered, and Fargo heard one word: "Terry."

Then the eyes went glassy, and the youth was dead.

Fargo dug three graves, and after he had filled in the earth, he leaned upon his shovel and deliberated.

Terry? Who the hell was Terry? Why did he send three executioners after him? Why? He had never tangled with anyone called Terry. Still, this man must have had a hard grievance to send three such killers.

The answer had to lie back in Spoon River. And strangely, he had spent only thirty minutes there, buying supplies at the general store and having one or two lousy whiskeys at the saloon.

He packed the shovel in his saddlebag, threw a leg over the pinto. Then he felt a quick sense of satisfaction. He had never liked leaving unsolved the riddle of his forced encounter with the women. It had preyed in the back of his mind all the time he was on the trail. Now he had a second riddle to solve. Why a man called Terry had wanted him dead.

A grim smile settled on his face as he turned the pinto around and headed back on the trail toward Spoon River.

JOIN THE **TRAILSMAN** READER'S PANEL
AND PREVIEW NEW BOOKS

If you're a reader of TRAILSMAN, New American Library wants to bring you more of the type of books you enjoy. For this reason we're asking you to join TRAILSMAN Reader's Panel, to preview new books, so we can learn more about your reading tastes.

Please fill out and mail today. Your comments are appreciated.

1. The title of the last paperback book I bought was: _____
_____

2. How many paperback books have you bought for yourself in the last six months?
□ 1 to 3   □ 4 to 6   □ 10 to 20   □ 21 or more

3. What other paperback fiction have you read in the past six months? Please list titles: _____
_____
_____
_____

4. I usually buy my books at: (Check One or more)
□ Book Store   □ Newsstand   □ Discount Store
□ Supermarket   □ Drug Store   □ Department Store
□ Other (Please specify)_____

5. I listen to radio regularly: (Check One)   □ Yes   □ No
My favorite station is:_____
I usually listen to radio (Circle One or more)   On way to work /
During the day / Coming home from work / In the evening

6. I read magazines regularly: (Check One)   □ Yes   □ No
My favorite magazine is:_____

7. I read a newspaper regularly: (Check One)   □ Yes   □ No
My favorite newspaper is:_____
My favorite section of the newspaper is:_____

For our records, we need this information from all our Reader's Panel Members.
NAME:_____
ADDRESS:_____ZIP_____
TELEPHONE: Area Code (   ) Number_____

8. (Check One)   □ Male   □ Female

9. Age (Check One)   □ 17 and under   □ 18 to 34
□ 35 to 49   □ 50 to 64   □ 65 and over

10. Education (Check One)
□ Now in high school   □ Graduated high school
□ Now in college   □ Completed some college
□ Graduated college

As our special thanks to all members of our Reader's Panel, we'll send a free gift of special interest to readers of THE TRAILSMAN.

Thank you. Please mail this in today.

NEW AMERICAN LIBRARY
PROMOTION DEPARTMENT
1633 BROADWAY
NEW YORK, NY 10019